Fast Finish

Bill Swan

James Lorimer & Company Ltd., Publishers
Toronto, 1998

First publication in the United States, 1999

James Lorimer & Company Ltd. acknowledges the support of the Department of Canadian Heritage and the Ontario Arts Council in the development of writing and publishing in Canada. We acknowledge the support of the Canada Council for the Arts for our publishing program.

Cover illustration: Jeff Domm

Canadian Cataloguing in Publication Data

Swan, Bill, 1939-
   Fast finish

(Sports stories)
ISBN 1-55028-641-2 (bound) ISBN 1-55028-640-4 (pbk.)

I. Title. II. Series: Sports stories (Toronto, Ont.).

PS8587.W338F37 1998   jC813'.54 C98-932334-X
PZ7.S969898Fa 1998

James Lorimer & Company Ltd.,
Publishers
35 Britain Street
Toronto, Ontario
M5A 1R7

Distributed in the United States by:
Orca Book Publishers,
P.O. Box 468
Custer, WA   USA
98240-0468

Printed and bound in Canada

Contents

For Mr. D.
and all the runners
in the 40-kilometre club
at S.T. Worden Public School.

1

Running Away

As Noah Meyers stepped out the front door of the school, he adjusted the knapsack on his back. The April sun shone on his face. He liked that. He could smell the mud of the playground from the morning's spring rain. He liked that, too. What he didn't like were the two classmates who waited for him by the sidewalk.

"Well, if it ain't Meyers, class wimp," Ian Brant said with a laugh. "Got his homework all bundled up nice and safe."

Brant carried no books. His full-length black raincoat hung below his knees. He had shaved his head bald on one side; the other side had been shingled in layers.

Beside him, Neil Zeko laughed. He tilted his head back and kept his lower jaw still while making snorting noises through his studded nose.

"We should check it out," he said, chewing hard on his gum. This changed the laugh into a strange cough. "Maybe we're missing some homework."

He said this just as Noah tried to squeeze by the two bullies. Neil reached forward and pulled at the buckle that held Noah's backpack closed. Noah pulled away.

"My, now! Isn't he touchy?" sneered Ian. "And we're just trying to help."

Noah spun around to confront Neil. As he did, Ian slipped behind him and made a quick grab at the backpack.

"Hey! Lookee here! We have geography homework!" Ian said, holding up a handful of loose-leaf pages he had ripped from the pack. "It's a good thing Noah reminded us!"

"Give those back!" Noah cried. He knew he sounded whiny, though he tried not to.

"What is it, Meyers?" taunted Neil. "Don't want to share with your classmates?"

The two circled Noah, moving away from the school, out of sight of any teachers crossing the parking lot. When he pivoted to face one, the other edged around behind him. "Give me my books!" he yelled. Noah could feel the lump in his throat, the tears close to the surface. Please, he thought, don't let those tears come now.

Noah stood taller than Neil. But what Neil lacked in size and strength he made up for in attitude. Ian, on the other hand, was larger than Noah. While Noah was thin, wiry, and strong, Ian was big, heavy — almost soft looking — and deceptively powerful.

Ian slipped behind Noah and reached a hand into the knapsack. Out came a math text.

"I need that!" Noah yelled, grabbing it back with a quick lunge before Ian could move. Noah clutched the math book under his left arm and moved sideways down the sidewalk, edging away from his two tormentors. At the same time, he shifted his pack off his left shoulder and tucked it in his right arm, holding it close to his body. The spring breeze chased his geography notes down the street. He gave up on them.

"Aren't 'cha gonna wait for the bus?" chanted Neil. "It's a long way home to your mom-meee!"

"Yeah," echoed Ian. "Come on back and we'll finish this discussion!"

Noah clutched at his book and his pack and began to run down the sidewalk, away from the pair.

"Wim-py, wim-py, wim-py," the two voices chanted after him.

Noah sprinted for the first few metres. He knew they wouldn't chase him. In a way, he hoped they would. He could outrun anyone he knew. That was one thing Noah Meyers could do: run. From bullies like Ian Brant and Neil Zeko. He had lots of practice.

By the time he reached the first corner, Noah had slipped his pack on his back. With his math text still tucked under his left arm, he shifted the load until he could control the bouncing by pushing down with his right elbow. It was awkward, but he could run, easily.

To avoid the bullies, or other classmates, Noah jogged up the hill past the high school, then south to the highway. On the way, he passed the new community centre, with its library full of new-smelling books, and swimming pool with the corkscrew slide. Along the highway, the sidewalk was new, separated from the four-lane roadway by a metre-wide strip of sod freshly laid that spring. Noah liked running along this walkway. Few others used it. He could run, alone, and that's the way he liked it.

Once he caught his stride, his lean legs churned in an easy rhythm. Run-ner, run-ner, run-ner, the stride said to him — but that was a fantasy he kept to himself.

After several blocks, Noah heard a horn sound a quick double bleep, like a friendly wave. The vehicle, a nine-passenger van with windows, had the name of Noah's family's store, Fast Finish, written on its side. His mother's brother, Max, waved from behind the wheel. Noah motioned his uncle on; he would see him at home.

His anger had gone before he turned onto Centrefield Road. Running did that, too. Once he got into that zone, his legs churning, his lungs pulling in air, everything else leaked out of his body.

* * *

Returning home that afternoon, Noah dashed in the side door. His mother sat at the kitchen counter, account books and bills from the business spread out on the table in front of her. With her brother, Max, she ran a store which sold used sporting equipment. This was, as she said, 'her afternoon to do the books.'

Max stood by the sink, filling his mug with fresh coffee. He was thirty-four, and smiled most of the time. His rumpled clothes almost hid the softer look extra pounds had given to his once-lean body. It was hard to tell if his hair was naturally curly or just uncombed. Because of the store he shared with his sister, he practically lived at the Meyers' house.

"School okay?" asked Mrs. Meyers. She wore her darkening blond hair pulled back into a bun. Her blue eyes did not smile as much as they once did. Before.

"Hmm. S'okay," Noah replied. "These books're really heavy."

"Saw that Zeko kid waiting by the bus stop near the school," Max said. "There's trouble, I can tell you. He's been a problem this year in the store."

Mrs. Meyers adjusted a pile of cheques on the counter. "It happens at their age. His parents' divorce last year didn't help."

"And the company he keeps! He came in the shop the other day with another kid … "

"Likely Ian Brant," Noah said, dropping his knapsack on the kitchen floor.

"Yeah, I think that was it. What a pair. They were looking for a used skateboard."

Max turned from the counter. "Don't look now, Noah, but you're losing some of your work." He pointed to the loose-leaf pages protruding from Noah's knapsack that Ian Brant had left in his grab for the geography notes. "You should do that thing up properly."

"You'd be better off to take half that stuff out of there," Mrs. Meyers said, nudging the backpack with her toe. "That thing must weigh a ton. I don't know how you manage."

Noah knelt by the pack, pushed his math text back inside and refastened the buckle. "Careless of me," he said. He wasn't going to tell his mother or his uncle about Zeko and Brant. They'd just make a big fuss and make everything worse, he thought to himself.

"Saw ya running up the street," Max said. "Racing somebody?"

"Donovan Bailey," Noah replied. "I won."

"Pigs fly, too," said Adam, as he crashed through the kitchen door from outside. Adam, ten years old, was Noah's younger brother. He came up to Noah's chin, but already you could see he would someday outgrow his brother. When he was happy — which was most of the time — he wore a smile so large you could count his back teeth. His baseball cap, with the peak pointed behind his right ear, covered his dark brown hair. He carried a baseball glove over his left wrist. His free hand removed the lid to the cookie jar, disappeared inside it, and came out empty.

"Baker on strike?" he asked, adding, before anyone could respond, "Can I have a cup of coffee?"

Mrs. Meyers seldom baked. Max, however, dropped by regularly, and kept them supplied with his homemade chocolate chip cookies.

"Not on your life," said Max. "Let me catch you drinking coffee and I'll tar you. It'll keep you outta the big leagues for sure."

Adam lived for baseball. He would, as his uncle Max said, give his right leg to play in the big leagues someday.

"That's silly!" said Adam. "We got store-bought cookies?"

Max snickered. "Store-bought?" he replied. "You would resort to eating store-bought cookies? After tasting my very own chocolate chip?"

"Starving people will eat rocks," Adam replied. Then he turned to Noah. "Want to play catch?" he asked, tossing him a glove.

Noah shrugged. He had once played minor baseball. He could run well, but was clumsy in the field. He had given it up the season before their father died. That had been two years ago. Now, Noah felt the need to look after his little brother. "Race you to the park!" he said.

The park was only half a block away and it was no race, even though Noah did slow down. The baseball diamond dominated the low end of the park, with a five-metre steep slope behind the backstop screen for bleachers. Behind the fence that ran parallel to the baselines on each side was a players' bench: a three-metre long bench almost a metre high, so high the minor league players had to jump to seat themselves. When they finally did, their young legs would dangle harmlessly in the air. The diamond itself had been built of crushed limestone, packed by thousands of feet over time into the smooth texture of concrete. Noah was standing in the middle of the diamond, tossing the ball up and down, by the time Adam arrived, puffing.

* * *

When the boys returned from the park there was a telephone message waiting for Noah.

"It's Bill Judge of the Viking Track Club," said his mother. "He would like you to call him right back. He wants to talk to you about joining the Vikings."

"The Vikings?" Noah replied. "You're kidding!"

Max drained his coffee cup. "I talked to him earlier this week," he said. "I told him you were interested in running, and mentioned your result at the school track meet. He said the club's always looking for sprinters who have the dedication to work hard. You interested?"

Noah hesitated. He loved to run; he would often daydream about running, about winning races.

"I've never run in a real race before," Noah pointed out.

"He says that doesn't matter. He says it'll take a while to train you. You stick with it, he said you'll be in fine form within a year. You start high school in the fall. The competition will get stiffer."

Mrs. Meyers rested a hand on Noah's shoulder. "I've signed Adam up for minor league ball this year. I think running track would be good for you. You can't sit around all summer and do nothing."

Noah expected he could, but didn't say anything. Still, he thought, it would be great to be with people who did not think runners were freaks.

Nervously, he picked up the phone and pushed the buttons, almost afraid to hope. The Vikings were the best — the fastest track club in all of Clarington, perhaps in all of Durham Region. The Clarington Vikings. This was a dream come true. A scary dream.

2

The Track Club

The next Saturday morning, it was a nervous Noah who arrived at the Oshawa Civic Fields carrying a small sports bag. In it he had his shorts, a T-shirt, and his only pair of running shoes.

The Civic Fields consisted of a football field surrounded by a 400-metre track. To one side, covering the length of the field, an unshaded grandstand provided seating. The stadium, with its track and football field, were only part of a complex that included three soccer fields, a swimming pool, an all-year indoor track with three tennis courts, and an auditorium and hockey rink. The auditorium was home of the Oshawa Generals, the junior hockey team of Bobby Orr and many other hockey stars. The Clarington Vikings, like many nearby clubs, trained in Oshawa because few other communities offered such facilities. A new community of subdivisions, farms, and small towns like Bowmanville, Clarington provided only rough cinder tracks at high schools.

Noah walked through the open gate and along the strip of grass in front of the grandstand. On the track, five groups of runners, in twos and threes, jogged easily. On the infield, another dozen or so flexed muscles in stretches. One guy, in tank top and Afro, repeated knee lifts down the field.

Noah recognized Bill Judge from his newspaper pictures. He was an average height, and had the build of an athlete. His black hair was parted precisely along the left side, but grew shaggy over both ears. His sideburns belonged in a rock-and-roll museum. He wore neatly pressed slacks and a golf shirt. His expanding middle pressed on the white belt of his slacks. In his hand he carried a clipboard, and sunglasses with a mirrored finish hid his eyes.

"You must be Noah," he said, as Noah approached. "Your uncle told me about you."

Noah had planned a glib reply. Instead, he just mumbled something in his nervousness.

"What we're going to have you do this morning is get acquainted, get to know our routine," Judge said. "Although the first thing you'll find is that your school races won't count for anything."

Noah blinked. His school track meet had been run on courses laid out on the playground, with no stopwatches and shorter-than-normal distances. He didn't expect they would impress anybody.

Judge pointed to the grandstand. "You can use dressing room *H* under the stands. Down the far steps and first door on the left. You get changed and I'll meet you back here."

Under the grandstand, the dressing rooms reeked of wet concrete. Dressing room *H* could hold a football team and smelled like it had. Several other guys had hung their clothes on the hooks and tucked their street shoes under the bench. Noah changed quickly, wondering what would happen if he couldn't keep up with the others.

Back on the field, Bill Judge was waving his clipboard at a pair of runners and hitching up his white belt. "Knees up! Knees up! That's better." Then he turned his attention to Noah.

"Your uncle tells me that you love to run," he said. "That's a good sign. Don't expect instant results. Are you ready to work at it?"

Noah mumbled his agreement. It was hard to make eye contact with someone wearing aviation sunglasses. Noah couldn't decide if he liked the man or not.

"The Vikings have three different groups. I coach the sprinters, so you don't even need to know about the others. Sprinters do the 100-metre dash, the 200-metre, the 400, and the 800. Two laps around the track is 800 metres. The 400-metre is one. You get the idea? We'll eventually figure out which is your best event."

"At the school track meet I ran everything."

Judge shifted his clipboard and pointed toward the track. "At this level, you have to specialize. We have two other groups. See those two groups out there on the track, jogging along? Those are the endurance runners. They run the 1500-metre, the 3000, 5000 — some of the older ones the 10,000. That's twenty-five times around this track, enough to drive anyone crazy. John Buchan, there, he's their coach." Judge pointed to an older man jogging around the track with the first group, chatting and laughing as they passed. "We also have several field events," Judge continued, as he started to walk. But the field coach isn't here today."

They approached a group of four, two guys and two girls, all about Noah's age. "Listen up, people. This is Noah. Noah, this is Jason, Melissa, Mandy, and Ryan. Noah, you'll go through warm-ups with this group. Later, we'll run a few drills just to see how you do."

Judge moved away, then turned back one more time. "And heed me: none of that trash-the-new-sprinter stuff, okay? Don't go out and try to crush him the first day." He consulted his clipboard as he shuffled off to the next group on the field.

Mandy, a light-haired thirteen-year-old girl with hazel eyes, spoke first. "What event do you run?"

"I don't know yet. Mr. Judge says he'll figure that out."

"Judge," said Ryan. He wore sunglasses and an Afro hair-cut. "You should call him Judge, everyone else does. And I hope you don't intend to run 100s. I run 100s."

"Don't pay any attention to him," said Jason. He had close-cropped blond hair and, even at thirteen, he was bigger and stronger than the rest. "He's just afraid you're better than him."

"I am not, Jason Bitters. I'm going to win a chance at the regional finals this year. That's more than you can say."

"Yeah, but we've got to earn it," added one of the girls.

Melissa shook her dark brown ponytail and smiled. Even at twelve, she was the group leader. "Ignore them," she said. "They'll spend the whole day grumbling and forget to run. Can we begin our warm-up now?"

The first item was a two-lap jog around the track. Noah ran beside Jason. The other three mumbled and complained a few metres behind.

At the end of the first lap, the groans increased. "This is the worst part of our workout," said Ryan. "Coach, he says this is to warm up our muscles — stretch 'em so we don't get injured. Me, I think it is just one big pain in the butt."

"You got it right there," said Mandy, from behind.

Noah found the warm-up laps easy, the pace slow. He was feeling he could jog all day when another group glided by. They were chatting easily, yet passed Noah's group without effort.

"Distance runners," said Ryan with a smirk. "That's all they do is warm up."

"Yeah, they do that all morning," said Jason. "They must be sick. Anyone that skinny must be sick."

"Careful what you say, Jason," said Ryan. "Noah here ain't no fullback."

Noah glanced around at the others. For the first time he was aware that, compared to them, he was lean. Well, he thought, maybe the track workouts would help add some muscle. He jogged easily through the last of the two warm-up laps.

"Ahh! Stretches!" sighed Jason, as he and Noah stepped onto the infield. "Say! What is the difference between a relaxed stretch and a nap?" He gestured to Noah.

Noah pondered for a moment, and shrugged. "I don't know."

"Give up?"

"Yeah. I guess."

Jason stretched out on the grass on his back, his eyes closed. "There is no difference," he said, arms behind his head, snorting snoring sounds with his nose.

The whole group dropped on the infield, like rag dolls with the stuffing falling out.

Noah followed the others in stretches — hamstring, quadriceps, knee lifts — then a shuffle on the track that was a combination of a knee lift and a skip. Noah's feet kept getting tangled.

Back on the track they practised starting from the blocks.

"Okay. Everybody loose?" It was Bill Judge again, clipboard in his left arm, sunglasses reflecting an egg-shaped track. "Then let's try a few repeats."

For the next half hour, the group ran and re-ran 100-metre dashes down the straightaway in front of the grandstand.

"Pump those arms! Lift those legs! Pump! Lift! Pump! Lift!"

Each time Judge signaled the start, Noah came up out of the blocks, knees high, arms pumping. Each time, by halfway down the stretch, he was four full metres behind the others.

Ryan always placed first. Mandy usually nipped into second, with Jason and Melissa close behind. At the finish, Noah glided across, four metres back. Seven times they ran the heat. Seven times Noah pulled up dead last.

"Good workout," Judge said to Noah as they finished up. "You got a lot of stuff to improve. Keep at it. Workouts are every Tuesday and Thursday at four and Saturday morning at nine. Unless, of course, there is a track meet."

Noah had never before thought that something as much fun as running could be so much work.

3

No Pain, No Gain

One Sunday afternoon, two weeks later, Noah slouched on the family room couch at the rear of the Meyers' split-level home. He stared vacantly at the television set.

"You look," said Mrs. Meyers, passing through the room, "like a zombie. Glassy eyes." She waved her hand before Noah's eyes. "Anybody home?"

"Leave me to my aches and pains," replied Noah.

The family room was at the back of the house, down seven steps to a finished basement level, with large windows that looked out on the backs of the flowerbed. On the walls hung a variety of family pictures: Noah and Adam as infants, Noah's first day of school, Adam with a fish, Adam and Noah with their father. In one corner stood an unused wood-burning stove. The television dominated the centre shelf of an oak entertainment unit. A photographic portrait of the boys' father, unsmiling in a business suit, hung on the wall between the television and the stove. Above it hung a wicker garland.

Noah's uncle Max appeared out of nowhere, and dropped onto the couch beside him. "Hurting a little from athletic endeavours, are we?"

Max was always popping in. Popping in was what he did best. He lived five kilometres away in an apartment. Noah knew it was five kilometres: once, on a dare, he ran the whole way.

"While you're up," he said to Noah, who was not up but still rather sprawled, "could you rustle up a cup of coffee for your aging uncle?"

Noah glared a fake killer-doom look. "Caffeine is a drug. My coach has forbidden me to touch it. 'Don't ever touch anything with caffeine in it. Coffee, tea, cola.' That's what he said. So sorry. I can't help you."

Max lifted both hands to the ceiling. "What ever happened to child labour?" he asked. "What ever happened to respect for the wisdom of age, to subservience, to child slavery?"

Adam half walked, half jumped down the steps from the kitchen level and into the family room. He wore shorts, a Blue Jays' T-shirt and cap, and bare feet. The left side of his face was scraped and bruised.

"I'll make you a cup," he said to Max. "As long as I can have one, too."

"Hey, whoa! What happened to you, little slugger? You look as though you took a bath under a street cleaner. And no, you can't, I'll make it myself."

"I slid home, head-first," Adam replied, as Max headed for the kitchen.

"Looks more like face-first."

"I scored the winning run. I'm like my dad — I'm a shortstop who steals bases."

Noah shifted uncomfortably. "One more winning run and you'll have used up your whole face."

"Thanks, big brother," he said, with a disparaging twist in his voice.

"When you're through being a hero, it's your turn to fold laundry."

"Just don't bug me."

With Mrs. Meyers working more than full-time hours at the store, both boys helped with regular chores. And everyone in the family agreed, laundry was a chore.

Shortly, Max returned with a mug of coffee. Mrs. Meyers came in and took a chair at her oak roll-top desk in the corner.

"These teams aren't too much for you two, are they?" she asked. "I mean, here we have Adam with one side of his face caved in, and Noah hobbling around, stiff and sore, awake half the night with cramps in his legs —"

"It's that bad?" asked Max.

Noah made a sour face. "Not every night. But yeah. Sometimes I get bad cramps at night. I tried to talk to the other kids about it, but they just laughed."

"What does the coach say?"

"No pain, no gain."

"Sounds like Bill Judge. From what I hear, he'll give lines like, 'When I was your age, we carried 100-pound sacks of wet granola up and down stairs.'"

"Something like that. He said my body will adjust."

"I went to high school with Judge, back when he was a track star. He was in grade eleven when I started grade nine." Max sat on his end of the couch and thrust his legs out into the room. He blew over the surface of the coffee cup, then slurped.

"Bill Judge?"

"Doesn't look all that fit now, does he? Just shows you."

"He's a tough coach."

"Tough in a coach doesn't hurt. How's your speed coming? You able to keep up with the others yet?"

Noah shrugged. "The only thing I seem to be able to do faster than any other sprinters is my warm-up laps. But when we start sprinting, I just can't move my legs fast enough."

"It'll come," said Mrs. Meyers.

Dragging himself off the sofa, Noah sat back down on the floor and worked into a hurdler's stretch. "It better. You just spent $250 on shoes and a track suit."

The racing shorts and top, in blue and orange, had been ordered through Fast Finish. The store specialized in used equipment: hockey skates and equipment, baseball gloves, bicycles, and new and used team uniforms, including racing outfits and warm-up suits for the Clarington Vikings. Noah's parents and his uncle Max had started the store several years before. After his father had died two years ago, Max and Mrs. Meyers had continued it as partners.

Adam stood by the wood stove, chewing on a wad of gum, slapping a baseball into his glove. Ker-slap! Ker-slap! "I could get you a crutch," he said. "Then you could go in three-legged races."

"And I could borrow some of Mom's makeup, too. And we could make one side of your face look almost human."

"It'll heal," Adam said, referring to his face rash. "It'll heal."

"So how do you spell that, h-e-e-l?" replied Noah.

"Stop acting like an older brother!" said Adam.

Max looked at his watch. "Hey, guys. I gotta go. Promised Jamie I'd be at the store by four. You want to come along?" He turned to his sister. "That be okay?"

"I could pick them up before dinner," said Mrs. Meyers.

"Let's go."

Fast Finish was located in a strip plaza eight blocks away on Highway 2. Beside it, the fumes of a small pizza shop sharpened Noah's appetite. Other nearby stores included a variety store, a sports bar, a sewing centre, and a sandwich shop.

The buzzer sounded as they opened the door. Windows ran across the full width of the store front, stuffed with seasonal displays. The direct sunlight of the afternoon blared through. The fluorescent overhead lights could not compete with the sunlight, so the shop always gave the impression of being cool and dark.

"Anything new?" Max asked the young employee behind the counter.

"Naw," said Jamie. "Couple of kids looking for skate-boards, that's all."

Along one wall of the store, racks of new bicycles hung from the ceiling. The opposite wall held row after row of ice skates and in-line skates, all used. A kayak decorated the wall at the rear of the store; a canoe tipped precariously in a perch near the ceiling. Hockey and lacrosse sticks, badminton, tennis and squash rackets, and a variety of golf clubs filled two display rows. Pads for elbows, heads, shoulders, kidneys, knees, and hips could be purchased for any sport, any time of year. The huge room smelled of leather, grease, and sweat.

Max made his way to the small office at the back. An old 486-model computer sat on a typewriter table. A battered desk was covered with invoices and bills, neatly stacked. Several pictures of runners decorated the walls.

"Remember those?" Max asked, nodding his head.

"Yeah. Those were … here before."

"You haven't been here for a while," Max said. It wasn't a question, just an observation.

Noah shrugged.

"Not since your dad died."

Noah looked through the open office door for Adam, but he was involved in an animated talk with Jamie at the front of the store. About baseball, of course. Jamie was finishing his last year of high school, and played baseball with at least two teams.

"These were your dad's pictures. I had forgotten about them until this track thing. See that one? That's Jerome Drayton, one of Canada's best marathoners, ever. That's him finishing the Metro Toronto Zoo twenty-kilometre run in — what — about 1976. Autographed," Max added. "And this one's Bruce Kidd. Your dad met him at a fun run in Toronto, I think he said with the Longboat Club."

"Longboat?"

"Named after another of Canada's great distance runners, Tom Longboat. Bruce Kidd wrote a book about him. Your mother has that at home somewhere."

"Wow."

Max flipped through some papers on the desk. "Track's a good sport. But in this country, everybody's full of hockey and baseball, hockey and baseball. Like Adam, there."

"I like running because you do it alone."

"Your mother ever tell you how this store got its name?"

"Nope."

"Well, our parents came from Finland. You want to be thankful you don't have a last name like Uuksulainen. That's what your mother and I grew up with. Anyway, when we first started the store with your dad, our parents loaned us some of the money, so we named the store Fast Finnish. You know, kind of a play on finish, with one *N*, and Finnish, with two."

"Kinda corny."

"You bet. Plus, nobody got it. So we finally cut out that second *N*. But if you look at the sign outside, you'll notice it's still there."

"Cool."

"I have one more picture around here somewhere," Max said, still rifling through the desk drawers. "Oh, here it is." He brought out a standard-size photo, nine centimetres by twelve centimetres, of two men, both bearded, in running shorts and tops.

"That's my cousin, Tim. He ran one afternoon with Lasse Viren."

"Who's he?"

"Viren? He won gold medals in the 5000- and 10,000-metre in the Munich Olympics in 1972 and doubled again at Montreal in 1976. His first medal was won in a world record time, even after falling early in the race. Great runner."

"From Finland?"

"How did you guess?"

Adam ran the length of the store and bounced through the office doorway. "Uncle Max, can I go with Jamie to the SkyDome to watch the Blue Jays play?"

"That's something you'll have to ask your mother."

"Yeah, but she won't let me. You might. Come on."

"Sorry, sport. That won't work."

"But it's for tonight. The game starts at 7:30. We'd have to leave now."

Clarington was an accumulation of new subdivisions that straddled the expressway east of Toronto. With no traffic, you could drive to the SkyDome from the Clarington-Oshawa border in about an hour. It took an hour and a half, with heavy traffic.

"Phone your mother."

"She'll say no."

"Likely, but if you don't phone the answer is still no. If you phone her, there's always a small chance ..."

"Okay, okay."

Adam dialed the phone, mumbled into the mouthpiece, argued once, then hung up. "Told you she'd say no," he said.

"So now you know." Turning back to Noah, Max added, "There's one more picture around here I want to dig out." Max pushed aside some boxes in the corner at the far side of the desk. A parade banner — two smooth round poles with a banner stretched between them — had been propped up in the corner.

"Our store banner for the Santa Claus parade float," Max said, as he lifted it aside. "Ah, here we are."

What he revealed was an old colour photograph, held in a cheap plastic frame. "You can have this if you want it." Max handed the picture to Noah.

Noah took the frame, rubbed the glass with his sleeve, and held it up to the light. In the photograph, a young man, his face contorted in the agony of effort and his eyes hidden by reflective sunglasses, stretched across the finish line of a race. He was young, late teens maybe, fit and lean.

"That's Bill Judge."

Max nodded. "Look closer."

The picture had been taken across the finish line looking toward the infield. In the foreground, an older man had stood in front of the photographer, almost blocking the shot, his hands gripped in tight fists, his face contorted in a scream.

In the background, his toes on the infield grass right on the finish line, another young man, perhaps in his early twenties, was frozen forever with his right hand crunching down on a stopwatch.

It was Noah's father.

4

Always Trailing

Even on a cloudy day, Bill Judge still wore his aviation sunglasses. Like mirrors, the lenses reflected the track, the runner, the clouds, but revealed nothing of the man behind them.

"For a warm-up today," he said, pointing to the oval track with his clipboard, "I want you to do four laps. Later …"

"Four laps … without … stopping?" asked Ryan.

"Four laps without stopping," Judge repeated. "We need to build a little endurance. That's what else warm-up jogs do. Build your endurance. And today you're going to need it."

"I don't like the sounds of this," Mandy whispered. When she smiled you could see the braces on her teeth. Her hazel eyes sparkled. At 13, she could out-sprint most boys.

Bill Judge overheard her and turned once more. "You shouldn't like the sounds of it. We're going to be doing a couple of 800-metre runs, and I'm being the toughest coach the world has ever seen." Behind his sunglasses, it was hard to tell whether his eyes were laughing or not. Then he broke into an uncharacteristic grin. "I've got workouts nobody's ever run yet," he said.

On the track, Noah ran with Mandy. The warm-up laps, as usual, were slow, plodding, and certainly done with little enjoyment. At least, none that showed.

"You hear that?" said Noah, from behind. "We have to do 800-metre paces today. Man!"

"That's twice around this track," said Jason, running a hand through his short hair. "Twice around this track at racing speed!"

Noah didn't feel that would be too bad, but dared not say so.

Ryan grimaced. "It's only the second lap that really hurts," he said. They were halfway around the first turn, jogging the warm-up laps. Noah closed one eye and tried to line up the closest goal post with another at the far end of the field.

"At least I might have a chance to get up to full speed," Noah said.

Three other runners pulled up behind them on the track.

"Excuse us," said the older man with them. "Would you mind if we joined you for warms?" Noah recognized John Buchan, the distance running coach. He wore a baseball cap on his balding head, and gold wire-rimmed glasses. He had very hollow cheeks. Three distance runners, one boy, two girls, all about thirteen, maybe fourteen, accompanied him.

"We're only going four laps," said Ryan. "That's hardly enough for you guys to work up a sweat."

"A lap is a lap," Buchan said. When he smiled, the sun caught the reflection of a silver-capped tooth. He had a benign, grandfatherly look. In spite of that, he moved easily around the track with the younger runners. Noah tried to imagine Bill Judge running beside the sprinters.

"Do you always run with the people you coach?" Noah asked.

"Just the warm-ups," he replied, smiling again. "When we start doing intervals somebody has to do the hard work and run the stopwatch."

"Oh, yeah, Coach," said one of the distance runners Noah recognized as Marc Ascott. Ascott was tall and lean, with dark curly hair. His picture had appeared in the local paper last year when he ran in the finals for a race.

One of the girls with Buchan spoke next. "Next time I'll run the stop watch and you run the intervals."

Noah recognized her, too. She was Diane White, and he had also seen her picture in the sports pages. Both she and Marc Ascott had made it to the provincial finals earlier in the month.

The second of the distance runners, a taller girl, interjected. "If you could see how this guy runs, you wouldn't say that," she said. "In his spare time he runs marathons."

"How far's that?" Noah asked.

"Twenty-six miles," replied the girl. "Twenty-six miles without a stop."

Ryan spoke up from a few metres behind. "That sounds like a cruel joke," he said. "I get tired riding twenty-six miles in a car."

Buchan shrugged. "You think running twenty-six miles is bad. You should try running forty-two kilometres."

"Same thing, isn't it?"

"Aw, you caught me," Buchan laughed.

"We know better than to try a distance like that," said Ryan. But his voice came from farther back. Noah glanced over his shoulder. He was running beside Buchan. The two other distance runners were two strides ahead. The sprinters, Melissa, Mandy, Ryan and Jason, had fallen back four or five metres.

"Hey, slow it up," Buchan said. "We're losing some runners here." He slowed his pace, letting the sprinters catch up. "Save your speed for your races."

In spite of the effort to slow down, Noah ran the four warm-up laps with Buchan and his runners. Noah started the fifth lap without realizing he had done so. Then Ryan yelled.

"Hey! Meyers! You gone soft in the head or what?"

Almost reluctantly, Noah rejoined his group on the infield grass for stretches. Bill Judge joined them.

"Okay, everybody," Judge said. "We've all limbered up, done a few strides, got those muscles all working in great shape, eh?"

"My arthritis is cramping me up," cracked Ryan. "I think I better sit this one out."

"Nice try, Ryan. No way. Today we're going to run 300s or 400s, just to get everybody moving. Then we're going to do an 800. Anybody not done that before? Just Meyers? Great. Let's move."

The 100s followed the same pattern as always. Noah came stumbling out of the blocks, fell behind, and never caught up. Last. Always last.

Finally, Judge gathered them together.

"Last item for the day. The 800. Twice around the track. Noah, you just try to follow the others as best you can. Don't worry about getting too far behind. Just don't drop out. No matter how far back you get, keep plugging. I'm going to record times here today so we can see how much everybody improves by fall."

Noah nodded. He was not sure if this had been a putdown. Just don't drop out, he told himself. Do as well as you can.

"Okay. No starting blocks this time. Line up here." Judge pointed with his clipboard to a line on the track.

"Marks! Set! Go!"

Noah and his four fellow sprinters leaped forward, arms pumping, legs high, their powerful strides pushing them down the track. Halfway through the first bend, Noah trailed by four or five metres. Ryan and Mandy, as usual, led the way. Jason and Melissa followed, heads lifted, backs arched, straining.

By the 200-metre mark, halfway around the track, Noah followed the others by more than ten metres. He sucked in air, drinking deep gasps. He was no longer insulted by Judge's advice about quitting. Just finish, he thought. Just finish.

By the time Noah began the straightaway on the first lap, the other four were passing the coach, starting the second lap. Noah was twenty-five metres behind. His legs hurt, his lungs burned.

"Pump those arms! Lift those legs! Pump! Lift! Pump! Lift!"

Judge waved him on with the clipboard as he finished lap one. The others were well into the first bend.

Noah was beginning to run more easily. He had given up on the idea of catching the other runners. He focused on finishing. Some other time, he thought, he could worry about keeping up. If there is another time. Whatever made him think he could be a runner? he wondered.

As he entered the backstretch, he could still see the others ahead. Going, going ... no. Still ahead, but not quite so far ahead.

Down the backstretch, Noah moved forward, long legs churning, his breath deep, his lungs heaving. By the 200-metre mark, halfway through the last lap, John Buchan stood with his group of distance runners.

"Atta boy, Noah!'" he cheered. "Looking smooth, looking smooth. Now reel them in!"

Reel them in? Noah wasn't sure what the distance coach meant.

Ahead, on the last curve, Melissa and Jason had overtaken Mandy and Ryan. Mandy had fallen farther back. Now she was just ten metres ahead of Noah.

"If I could just catch one," Noah thought. Through the curve, his hair bouncing on top of his head, Noah closed in on Mandy. And Ryan. As he entered the final straightaway, he swung around and went by both the sprinters on the outside lane. Melissa and Jason were now ten metres in front. Nine metres. Reel them in, reel them in, Buchan said. Step by step, the leaders came closer. Was this what they mean by having others 'come back to you?' Noah wondered.

At the finish line, Noah trailed Melissa and Jason by three strides. Mandy and Ryan lagged behind him by five, six metres.

"That was 2:40!" Bill Judge, stopwatch in hand, flagged his finish with the clipboard. Then, while Noah bent over with his hands on his knees drinking air in gasps, Judge flagged the others to a finish.

"Ryan, 2:45! Mandy! 2:50! What, all you guys been eating lead chips?"

But the runners huddled by the track now, still gasping, trying to suck oxygen from the air. Would they ever breathe slowly again? Noah wondered.

Eventually, Judge urged them into a warm-down routine: light jogging once around the track, some stretches. Before he finished, Noah felt a hand on his shoulder. John Buchan grinned, his silver tooth gleaming in the sun.

"Great run!" he said. "I knew they'd come back to you. You kept your head. You're going to be a good runner."

For the first time in six weeks of training, Noah thought maybe he was right.

5

A Disappointment

The glow Noah felt after the 800-metre time trial lasted only until Tuesday's workout.

This time, Judge had switched the workouts to 200-metre repeats. Starting at the far side of the track, the runners were to sprint around the bend, a half circle, then head up the straight final stretch to the finish.

Noah liked this better than repeating 100 metres. The other runners still scampered ahead of him, though, pulling away from him right from start to finish.

Between repeats, the sprinters walked around the infield, stretching and shaking out muscles. "Relax, relax, relax," Judge bellowed. "Shake it out. The key is recovery. Get those muscles back for the next repeat."

Buchan and three or four distance runners jogged by on the track. They waved; Noah returned their smiles. He tried to picture his grandfather running with a group of teenagers. He couldn't.

"Okay, group, listen up." Judge propped his clipboard on his left hip. "Saturday is the Etobicoke all-comers' meet," he said. "We're going to be taking an impressive team so we can see how everyone works out in competition."

Mandy, Ryan, Jason, Melissa, and Noah crowded around. This time there were no wisecracks. They circled their coach in anticipation.

"Mandy, Ryan, we're going to run both of you in the 100-metre and 200-metre events. Get lots of rest, you'll need it. Jason and Melissa, I want you to run the 200 and the 400. You'll have plenty of time between events, so it is important for you to warm up properly each time." The sunglasses reflected one face after another. "Questions?"

"How do we get there, coach?" It was Ryan.

"We'll meet here at 8:00 o'clock Saturday morning," replied Judge. "I've got lots of room in my van."

"What about Noah?" asked Mandy.

"Yeah. I need to see you privately for a minute, Meyers." Judge jerked his head to one side, motioned with the clipboard.

Away from the others, Judge lowered his voice, dropped his gaze to the ground, and kicked at a clump of grass on the infield. "See, you're not quite ready for competition yet, Meyers," the coach said. "I don't want you going into a track meet and getting blown away. Right now, that's just what would happen. These others," he indicated Melissa, Ryan, Mandy, and Jason, "are going to get their eyes opened. Maybe that's what they need to really dig in there. But I don't want you getting discouraged. So you'll sit this one out. Okay?"

Noah nodded. He understood, but he still did not like it. "Do you think I'll ever be a runner?" he asked.

"What do you mean?"

"I mean, is all this worth the effort? It's been six weeks now. Am I going to make it?"

Judge shrugged. "You got some talent," he said. "But it'll take a year for us to find out. You gotta be patient." Then he turned on his heels and walked away.

* * *

That evening, Mrs. Jones phoned from across the street. She needed a baby sitter for Saturday, and wondered if Noah would be available.

Noah pondered. As a member of the track club, he felt he should go to the meet, just to cheer his teammates on and to become familiar with the atmosphere. "I'll phone you right back," he said.

He dialed Judge's number, then explained the situation. "I really would like to be there," he said. "I need to find out what it's all about. But I really, really need the money." Noah could hear the coach shrug over the phone.

"It's up to you. I think we might have room in the van. It really doesn't matter. You do what you think is best."

Thanks, Noah thought. That helps a lot.

Noah stared at the phone for a full minute before calling Mrs. Jones back. It doesn't matter. Was that what he had said? The remark stung. He told Mrs. Jones he would be available right after lunch. First, there would be the morning track workout.

After hanging up the phone, he remembered. With the track meet on Saturday, there would be no workout. Unless, of course, he went to the track by himself. Which maybe at this point was just what he needed. A morning to run the way he felt.

* * *

Noah expected the Civic Fields to be deserted on Saturday morning, but when he arrived, John Buchan was already on the track with one of the distance runners. Their voices drifted across the field, punctuated by bubbles of laughter.

A few minutes later, when Noah was standing on the edge of the infield adjusting his shoelaces, Buchan dropped away from his partner on the track and approached.

"Morning. You getting ready for a workout?"

Noah nodded.

"The sprinters are all away today," he said. "Track meet. You'll be alone."

"Coach Judge says I'm not ready. And I got a baby-sitting job this afternoon, or else I'd have gone with them anyway." Noah tied the last knot, tight. Some of his anger showed in the way he clenched his jaw.

"Working out alone is tough," Buchan said, after an awkward moment. "Care to warm-up with us?"

Noah stared at Buchan, then looked at the other runner jogging along the backstretch. "Yeah," he said at last. "I'd like that."

Thirty, or forty metres before the other runner reached them, Buchan motioned to Noah to start jogging. "It'll let you start slowly. He'll catch us," he instructed.

They began at an easy jog, bobbing slowly down the track. Buchan seemed in no hurry. Even so, it took the other runner a full lap before he had overtaken Noah and the coach.

Noah had just begun to breath deeply. Buchan talked, his voice unstressed, as though he had been out for a long walk rather than a run. Noah was surprised.

"Noah Meyers, this is Marc Ascott. Marc, Noah."

"Hi, guy," Ascott said, as he fell in, one half-step behind. He was a year older than Noah, dark-haired and slightly taller than Buchan. He ran with no shirt. Noah remembered him from his first day at the track. He was a star as a high school junior, and a month earlier had run in the provincial finals but Noah couldn't remember at what distance.

"Say, Coach," Marc said, "he runs pretty good. For a sprinter."

"Well," Noah replied. "Anybody can jog. Even grandfathers." Then, immediately, he wished the words back.

Buchan laughed. "I'll hit you with my cane," he said.

Ascott smirked. "You can get away with a crack like that," he said. "You're a guest. If John were your coach he'd get even with you at the next workout."

"Revenge," said Buchan with a smile. "And don't you forget it."

"Workout?" Noah repeated. "We sprinters do workouts 'til they hurt. But you distance runners call *this* a workout?"

Ascott snorted, trying to imitate derision. He failed, but Noah understood the intent. "This, dear Mr. Sprinter," he said, "is a warm-up, which is all we do today since we are racing tomorrow. Should you care to join us on Tuesday, I'm sure that Coach Buchan here would be glad to introduce you to the rigours of a distance runner's workout."

A few laps flew by, wordless. Noah broke the silence. "I'm trying to imagine Coach Judge doing a workout like this," he said. "He seems so attached to that clipboard."

Buchan replied, "You should have seen him twenty years ago. He was one of the best 200-metre runners around. That signal went off, he came flying around the bend like he was shot from a gun. He could hit that straightaway with the fastest finish around."

"He was that good?"

"Yup-per," replied Buchan. "I was his coach. That was back before I discovered the joy of distance running."

"He doesn't look like a runner now."

"It happens. I was like him in my thirties, added a few pounds. That's about when I started jogging to wear it off."

"I'm still trying to picture Bill Judge running," Noah said.

"One year he was runner-up for a provincial title. Now he's after one of his sprinters to win that title for him."

"Well," said Marc Ascott, "maybe the distance runners can get one for him this year."

Buchan laughed. "That'd be good for the club, but I don't think that's what Bill Judge has in mind. He's still a competitive cuss. For him, that provincial title is unfinished business."

"That's why he drives us sprinters so hard?" Noah asked.

"If I remember, I used to drive him pretty hard, too. He'll push hard to get a winner."

They ran together for twelve laps — almost five kilometres. Later, the three did some stretches on the infield. Buchan added a couple of stretches that Noah had not seen, including one similar to that done by a ballet dancer, with one leg up on a chest-high bar.

Afterward, Buchan dug into a portable cooler and produced a bag of ice. This he wrapped around his left knee, holding it in place with a tensor bandage. "Parts starting to rust out and fall off," he said. "The older you are, the worse it gets."

Ascott winked at Noah. "I hope your body has forgiven your teeth more than it has your hair."

Buchan ran one hand through his thin hair. "Could be worse," he said. "Would you like me better with thin hair and grey teeth or grey hair and thin teeth?"

While Noah tried to ponder that one, Buchan shifted the conversation. "Say, if you're interested, I'm taking Marc here, and Diane White, to a road race in Lindsay tomorrow. You'd be welcome to come along, if you wish."

Noah looked at him, then at Marc. "You mean just to watch?"

"If you'd like. It's a five kilometre course. About the same as we ran today. And there'd be a lot of joggers who would not run as fast as we did. Come on and run, if you're interested. It'd be a good off-track workout."

Noah thought of Judge and the team of sprinters. They were at a track meet, and wouldn't work out until Tuesday. Besides, maybe being with runners like Ascott and Diane White would be inspiring. "Sure," he said at last. "Why not? Sounds like it might be fun."

6

A Road Race

Lindsay is a small Ontario town northeast of Clarington. The road race started and ended at the fairgrounds. Buchan pulled his car into a parking spot on the grass. After the hour's drive, the runners were happy to uncoil their limbs and stretch.

"Wow! I've never seen so many runners!" said Noah.

Although it was still one hour until race time, the grounds had already half-filled with lean, fit racers: Young men and women in their twenties, runners in their thirties, forties, fifties, and even a few who looked older, possibly in their seventies or eighties. Do people run when they are that old? Noah wondered.

There were also lots of teenagers, mostly club members, like Noah, turned out in team colours. The Viking uniform consisted of royal blue shorts and a white top with flourescent orange trim. The word Viking was splashed across the top in the same ugly orange. Buchan had loaned the outfit to him because the sprinters had not yet provided him with racing colours. Noah wondered, though, if he should actually wear the outfit in public.

"Okay, gals and guys," Buchan said. "I'll pick up our racing kits. You scout the change rooms, the washrooms, and pick up a map of the racing course. Get yourselves oriented."

All around them, runners leaned over car fenders, sipping sports drinks from bottles and telling each other lies about their best races. Several groups were already jogging slowly by on the road and on the nearby sidewalk. It was still an hour before race time, but they were warming up already.

"They make me tired just watching," said Noah.

Marc Ascott laughed. "They'll jog slowly like that. Then, once their muscles are really warmed up and stuff, they'll stretch. Racing on tight muscles can get you injured. Ask me, I know."

Also with them was Diane White. She was a high school track senior, sixteen, blond, tall, racing lean, and fit.

"We've got lots of time before we start our warm-up," she said. "I'm going to scout out the change rooms." She grabbed her track bag from the trunk of Buchan's car and motioned to the grandstand.

The Lindsay Fairground was a monument to southern Ontario's rural history. A century earlier, the grandstand had been built to hold the annual fall fair. Now rickety, in spite of fresh paint, the structure could seat maybe a thousand people overlooking an 800-metre dirt track designed for the racing of harness horses.

Under the grandstand, modern plumbing had been added fifty years ago. The washrooms were, in fact, the change rooms.

Buchan had gone to pick up their entry packages; Ascott had disappeared with a group of runners he knew. Noah found himself alone in the men's washroom. The grungy wet concrete smelled of urine and chemicals. A toilet had overflowed into a floor drain. An orphan, rusting shower dripped behind a curtain in the far corner. Noah decided to look for better change facilities. He stepped out into the corridor.

"Ugh! Somebody's got to be kidding!" Diane White said, emerging from the women's washroom. "Is the men's as bad?"

Noah nodded. "Worse, I think."

Diane pulled at Noah's arm. "Come on, let's see what else we can find."

Across the highway and down the road 600 metres, they found a service station willing to allow them the use of washroom facilities.

Diane thanked the attendant and then emerged with a key. "One unisex washroom," she said. "We'll have to take turns standing guard outside. You do that and we'll be buddies forever."

Diane emerged five minutes later, ready to race. She handed the key to Noah. "Lock from the inside. I won't let anyone in." Quickly, Noah changed into shorts, racing top and running shoes.

"May we come back after the race?" Diane asked the attendant.

"Just don't tell the other 900 runners," he said, "or we'll be buried. My boss said we're not supposed to let any runners in."

"It's our secret," Diane said.

Back at the car, Noah and Diane studied the map of the race course that Marc had picked up. The start line was traced in lime across the dirt track in front of the grandstand. After almost a full lap, the course slipped through a gate onto the road, straight out almost two kilometres, and then doubled straight back. The last lap was to be run on the grandstand's dirt track.

"Hills?" Diane asked.

Marc shook his head. "Some of the guys who ran it last year said it's flat as a pancake, if you don't count the bridge. The worst part's likely to be the dust on the track."

"Oh, yeah. Great. Be a good idea to be up front at the start."

Noah looked over at the track. It was packed dirt and likely great for horses. In the dry July heat, the dirt had worn dry and powdery. "I was planning on jogging along at the back," he said.

Diane shrugged. "Somebody'll be there. But I'll bet it will be like following a big truck down a dry gravel road."

Already Noah could taste the dust and did not like it, not one little bit.

"You could always watch from the grandstand," Buchan said, approaching the car. He pulled out the race packages. "Your race bib is in there," he said. "One pin in each corner so it's high enough to be in view. There should be safety pins included. Don't jab yourself."

Noah carefully opened the package. It included the racing bib — the number 769 — and four safety pins, along with a brochure on "Lindsay, the vacation wonderland" and a photocopy of a story on last year's race from the sports pages of the local weekly newspaper. A yellow coupon offered a free sports drink following the race.

Noah stuffed everything but the race bib into his track bag, which he then placed in Buchan's trunk.

"Anything else?" Buchan asked, before slamming the lid. "Now, providing I do not lose the key, you can meet me here after the race to get your stuff."

"We have to wait that long?" asked Diane, smiling.

"This is not my day to set a personal best," Buchan said, "but I'll finish in twenty-three minutes and change. Anybody who finishes before that deserves to fry out in the sun. Good luck!"

With half an hour before the race's start, the four jogged slowly around the grounds, once around the track, and slowly up one tree-lined street. The area had now filled up with runners, officials, and spectators. Police had blocked off the running course, and late-comers found their access to the fairground parking lot restricted.

* * *

Noah's plan to fight the dust seemed simple. He would start the race as close to the front as possible, and stay near the front for the first 600 metres on the track. Then, when the dust settled behind them, he would slow his pace and jog the rest of the course. He thought it sounded great.

When the starting signal sounded, Noah stood in the third row back, beside Diane.

Immediately, they moved forward. For the first strides, the runners were packed so closely together that one mistake would trip a dozen. Noah focused on his footing. He had little time to think of his pace. There was no chance to think of falling back. The tide of runners carried him.

They reached the street within two minutes. Already the lead runners had stretched ahead, spreading the competitors out in a thinning line. Noah looked to his left, hoping to find Diane. No luck. He scanned the runners ahead, thinking she should be up there. He could see Marc Ascott, his dark, curly-haired head bobbing up and down, just behind the lead runners. But no Diane.

"Come on there, first girl! Way to go! Way to go!"

The spectators were cheering them on. Noah's eyes darted from runner to runner. First girl? he wondered. Then suddenly, Diane was running at his elbow.

"Relax," she said as she went by. "You've got a long way to go yet!"

They had left the dust behind, but slowing down didn't seem so important. Noah was breathing smoothly and his pace was even. The excitement of the race increased his adrenaline, carrying him effortlessly through the first kilometre.

At the one kilometre mark, a race marshal fixed her eyes on a stop watch and yelled out the time as each runner glided by. " … 3:45, 3:46, 3:47 … " she screamed.

Noah tried to calculate the time in his head. Five kilometres, four to go.

"Come on there, first woman! Way to go! Way to go!" The shouts were for Diane, ahead of him now by ten metres. Nobody looked to be moving terribly fast. But now Noah had begun to work hard for each step.

At the short, low grade on the Chapel Street bridge, Noah instinctively lifted his knees higher. Suddenly, they were heavy, sluggish tree stumps.

One runner, then two, went by.

"Keep it going!" one said, drifting by like a gazelle. "You're looking good. Keep it up!" And then was gone.

Noah drank air now, gulping. It was not a pretty sight. He wished he had slowed down when they left the dirt track. His lungs were beginning to burn. Maybe he should have eaten dust at the back of the pack, he thought.

The two kilometre mark came up.

" … 8:30, 8:31, 8:32, 8:33 … "

Somewhere in the last few seconds, dozens of runners had passed him. Ahead, the race course followed the street through a left turn. He could see Diane now, easily a full minute ahead of him. Her tall frame moved smoothly, passing male runners. In the club's running shorts and top she looked all legs, her stride smooth, unhurried. Until, Noah thought, you try to catch her. Hang on, he told himself.

Runners were now passing him constantly. Noah realized they had not speeded up — he had slowed down. Up or down? he wondered. Do runners slow up or slow down?

" ... 13:22, 13:23, 13:24 ... " the race marshal sang out. Three kilometres. Two more to go, Noah told himself.

His body hurt. He could drop out. Everyone would understand. Nobody expected him to finish well.

But he would finish, he told himself, even if he had to walk the last mile.

" ... 19:04, 19:05, 19:06 ... "

With one more kilometre to go, only a few runners were now passing. One, an older man with grey hair and 'You've just been passed by a GRANDFATHER' written on the back of his shirt, breathed in grunts.

Then Buchan was beside him.

"Great run!" he said. "Keep it smooth ... you'll finish ... fine."

Noah tried to explain.

"Started out ... too ... fast." He struggled to speak as he exhaled. The words came out in quick grunts.

"Jog it in," Buchan said.

Back near Chapel Street, they returned in the opposite direction over the same small bridge. The slow, short rise felt like a mountain. Buchan was yards ahead and moving out.

Marc and Diane had been right about the dust on the track. It swirled in little clouds and hung in the air until it was sucked in by unsuspecting lungs. Noah made the turn from the road to the raceway track, slowing almost to a walk. His legs hurt. His chest throbbed. Runners continued to pass him.

On the backstretch, however, a few came back. Midway through the backstretch, Noah found fresh legs. He surged, kicking in with a fast finish to pass thirteen runners in the last stretch, floating, floating, floating ...

" ... 24:19, 24:20, 24:25 ... "

He had finished — 24:25.

Marc and Diane helped Noah through the finish chute, where his number was recorded to be matched later with his finish time.

"I think you've just learned a lesson," Diane said, as they walked out the soreness, sucking on orange sections. The important thing in distance running is pace."

Half an hour later, the results were posted for all to see. Marc had finished sixth overall and first in the fifteen and under age group. Diane had finished twentieth, first in her age group, and first woman overall.

Noah was pleasantly surprised when he saw his own posting: 220th overall, tenth among boys thirteen and under, and good enough for a copper-coloured finisher's medal.

At the awards ceremony, someone handed him the medal and the mayor shook his hand. It was the first real running award he had ever won, and it softened some of the pain in his legs. He wondered what Bill Judge would say when he told him at Tuesday's workout.

7

Adam's Great Catch

The next day, Monday, Noah became busy with several jobs. In the morning, he baby-sat while Mrs. Wilson, two doors down from the Meyers' house, did her grocery shopping. In the afternoon, Mr. Kowalski, from one street over, was called in to work on his day off. He needed a sitter until Mrs. Kowalski returned from work about four, and Noah took the job.

Finally at home, Noah flopped on the family room couch.

"How's the great marathon king?" Adam asked, as he slouched into the room, baseball mitt and ball in one hand, cap on sideways and a slingshot in his right rear hip pocket.

Adam was three years younger than Noah, and for as long as either could remember, they had played together. Noah taught Adam to play video games, baseball, soccer, Monopoly, card games. They dug worms together, and Noah had helped Adam construct his ant farm.

Noah shrugged.

"Yuh comin' to my game tonight?" Adam persisted, the question punctuated by the fidgety snap, snap, of the bubble gum he was chewing. "I'd like you to come."

"Mmm? Sure. I think. Unless somebody else wants to give me many dollars to look after their kids. Money, money. I'll play with kids all day for money."

Adam threw himself into a chair, flicked on the television converter, flipped through six channels and then turned it off again.

"Bored?" Noah asked.

"Naw. Game day. And we're playing a tournament this weekend."

"Jitters? You could always do laundry."

"Did. Folding ain't that much fun."

"It's not supposed to be fun. It's supposed to be done. Fun, done. Get the rhyme?"

"And socks. I hate pairing socks."

"I bet you like wearing them in pairs."

"Very funny. Why can't all laundry be towels? They're the easiest to fold."

Noah watched as Adam kicked his left leg repeatedly against the side of the chair. He had never before thought of his little brother as the nervous type.

"I'll go to your game tonight … "

"Good. Thanks."

" … if you'll come to my track workout tomorrow."

"Yeah, but that's … "

"Blackmail? No, it's a swap. Deal?"

"Deal."

Despite the efforts of their uncle Max, Noah realized that he and his brother were moving apart. Had that started before their father got sick? he wondered to himself. Would it have been that way had he not died? Would they grow up and away from each other, maybe as adults live in different cities and see each other once a year at a family picnic or Christmas?

"Come on," he said. "Let's make a sandwich or something. Then you can get dressed for the game, and we'll bike over together. I'll toss a few with you to get you warmed up. Until the others get there."

* * *

That night, Adam stole three bases, hit two doubles and scored four runs to lead his team to victory. He became the team hero.

In the bottom half of the last inning, the opposing team had loaded the bases. Their clean-up batter, who had gone three-for-three that evening, came to the plate. Adam's team led by one run.

The slugger ripped a line drive toward a big hole in left centre field. The runners began to move, and the opposition bench exploded in cheers. Suddenly Adam, playing shortstop, ran three steps, leaped and pulled in an over-the-head catch for the third out, with the bases loaded.

The uproar on the opposing team's bench collapsed like a punctured beach ball. Adam's teammates, and the spectators behind them, rose in a roar.

Loudest of all the spectators was Noah.

"Yeah, Meyers! Attaboy Meyers! Waytogo, kid!"

If any of this embarrassed Adam, he did not let on. Compared to this, though, Noah thought, a track workout would be a really boring spectator sport.

8

Comparing Medals

Y ou did what?"

Bill Judge slapped his clipboard against his thigh repeatedly. Whack. Whack.

"I ... ran in a road race on Sunday," Noah replied. He tried to look the coach in the eye, but Judge never took off his sunglasses, so all Noah could see was himself looking back, and he looked frightened.

The coach let out a long, steamy sigh. "That was a darned fool thing to do."

"I thought ... "

"Coaches do the thinking, son. Coaches do the thinking. You do more things like that and you're going to get your slow twitch and fast twitch muscles all confused and you'll end up being a couch potato. Sprinters need fast twitch muscles. For power. For strength. For speed."

"But we jog in our warm-up, so ... "

"What did I say about thinking? Did it ever dawn on you why sprinters jog so slowly? Well, I'll tell you why. They're not trying to go fast. The warm-up jog is just that: a warm-up. To get muscles heated up, and loose, so you don't pull a hamstring when you're under power."

Noah glanced over to the grandstand in front of the track. Adam was swinging on the railing just under the *No Standing* sign. This was not exactly what he wanted Adam to see.

"You got that?"

"Pardon?"

"Meyers, no more distance stuff, got it? Any more dumb stuff like that and you won't be a sprinter and I won't coach you. Got it?"

"Yes, sir."

Judge smiled mechanically. "Great. Now get out there with the others and get warmed up."

Noah jogged across the field to join the other sprinters in the warm-up. They were bubbling with news of the Saturday track meet.

"Man! I just got blown away in that 100!" Melissa said, waving her arms as they jogged along the edge of the track. "Coach said I should do the longer sprints — 400 ... 800. But I told him I thought 800-metres is a long way."

Mandy ran two steps behind. "Yeah, but look how well you did in the eight."

Noah looked at Melissa, jogging at his left elbow on the inside of the track. "Well? How did you do?"

Melissa faked modesty. "Aw, shucks," she said. "I got a gold medal. I ran 2:32, and came in ... first."

Noah beamed in pride for her. "That's great! It sure must make all this work worthwhile. A gold medal!"

From behind them, Ryan spoke. "You shoulda seen her up there on the podium, just like the Olympics! They all sang our club anthem, and stood to attention. Then all day long people asked me if I were Melissa Radisson's teammate, and if they could have my autograph or an interview ... "

Melissa laughed. "You'll have to excuse Ryan," she said. "He exaggerates. No anthem. No autographs. But he did win a silver medal himself."

"And we did give our Viking yell," Mandy said.

The runners stopped in the middle of the track to form a circle.

"Vi-king! Vi-king! Vi-king!" they yelled.

"That's our race cheer, too," said Jason. "It speeds us all up. It's our secret weapon. Look what it did for Ryan."

"Yeah, 12.5 in the 100. Coach said I should be down to twelve seconds before the season's over. Now, eleven flat. That's what I'd call great."

"Ten flat would be even better," said Mandy. "Then you could run in the Olympics."

"And nine flat would set a new world record with plenty of time to spare," added Ryan. "A mark that'd last for a century or more."

On the second lap of their warm-up rounds, Noah scanned the grandstand for Adam. Finally he spied him, halfway up the grandstand, chin in his hands, looking as bored as possible. It was a mistake to invite him, Noah thought. A track meet, maybe. But the workout … ?

"Too bad you didn't get to come with us," said Mandy finally. "You'da beat some of the other runners, I'm sure. There was this one guy … "

"Yeah, like maybe in the 800," said Ryan. "You did well in that time trial here last week. Surely the coach'd let you run in something like that next time."

On their third warm-up lap, John Buchan, along with Marc Ascott, Diane White, and two other distance runners pulled up to pass.

"Beep! Beep! Roadrunners coming through!" said Diane. She smiled at Noah as she passed.

"Hi! I thought after Sunday you'd become a real runner and do distance," she said. Her smile was all white teeth and dimples.

"I have eaten enough dust for one season," Noah replied.

Buchan chuckled. "Don't tell your sprinter friends about your medal," he said. "They'll be jealous!"

"They're too busy talking about their gold and silver," Noah replied. Chatting with Marc and Diane, Noah was swept along into their warm-up pace.

From ten metres behind, Ryan yelled: "Hey, Meyers! Don't get carried away there. Coach still has some work for us to do!"

Oh, yeah, thought Noah. He slowed his pace, waving to the distance group. "See ya, guys."

The sprinter's warm-up pace now seemed sluggish. Noah dropped to the back of the group, beside Ryan. From here, the group looked to be trudging, one heavy footstep after another. Yet the coach had said this warm-up was to get the muscles loose. He knew these runners could sprint hard. Their powerful legs propelled them forward, building speed with each step. Noah wondered if he'd ever be able to sprint with them.

He had a hard time staying focused on the stretches and warm-up routine. Twice he waved to Adam, bored in his perch up in the grandstand. Noah would have no home run for him to cheer about in the bottom of the ninth.

The distance runners were running 800-metre intervals. From a distance, they didn't look fast. But watching them now, gliding by other runners, Noah could appreciate their speed. Not powerful speed, like a sprinter, but controlled, I-can-keep-this-up-longer-than-you-can speed. Buchan no longer ran with them. He stood by the side of the track, clipboard and stopwatch in hand. He wore no sunglasses.

"Hey! Meyers! Wake up, will ya?" Bill Judge yelled. He was louder than usual today, gruffer, more demanding. "Ya ever want to run fast enough to compete, ya gotta stay focused! All the time!"

"Sorry."

"If you wanta become a sprinter, ya gotta build power like a sprinter. Sprinters need power. Power in the legs. Power in the upper body. You ever see a distance runner with an upper body?"

The rest of the sprinters' group laughed.

Judge snapped them back. "Okay, enough of that. We got some work cut out for today. Ryan and Mandy, I want you both to work on your starts. Get the blocks, do repeats, ten strides out only. And remember, pull up slowly. We don't want you tightening up your quads!"

For Melissa and Jason, Judge had other orders. "The rest of you are going to do twos and fours. Four twos and two fours. Just one thing: don't sit down between 'em. Jog around, walk about, stretch, but don't sit. Got it? And wait for my signal to begin each repeat. I'll be up here by the finish line. 'Course, you'll start the 400s from there, so that's no problem. When you're doing the twos, wait for my signal."

Then, almost as an afterthought, Judge nodded to Noah, "You, too, Meyers."

* * *

After the workout, Adam won the bicycle race home. At the corner convenience store they stopped to pick up the loaf of bread their mother had requested. As they came out of the store, Ian Brant and Neil Zeko blocked their path. Zeko flicked a wad of chewing gum at Noah.

"If it ain't old fleet foot," he said. "Mr. Olympics."

"Yuh engaged to Diane White yet, Mr. Prissy?" scorned Rhonda Rogers. Rhonda chummed in the same group as Brant and Zeko. She wore black lipstick and white, pasty makeup. "Or does she even know who you are?" Rhonda snapped her gum in Noah's face. They all laughed.

"I'd thank you to let us by," Noah warned.

"Or what? You gonna sick muscle boy Adam on us?" Two or three other kids, slouched against the wall like rag dolls, laughed.

Rhonda tried to slip into position in front of Noah's bike. Noah saw the movement, and stepped twice to his left, putting a pedestrian between him and the tormentors. Quickly, both he and Adam swung onto their bikes.

"Creeps," Noah said as they cycled away.

"Real creeps," Adam repeated.

Behind them they could hear the taunting laughter.

9

The Distance Runner

"You want to do what?"

Judge pulled off his sunglasses. For the first time, Noah could see his penetrating blue eyes. He hesitated, then plunged forward.

"I want to run with the distance runners," he repeated. "I mean, I think I'm getting nowhere here. I'm just not a sprinter."

Judge adjusted his hat, drew his left wrist across his forehead. "Great, just great. Two months' work, then zip! Away you go. I don't understand. I just don't."

Noah persisted. "But after two months I'm not running those 100s any better. You've said it yourself — sprinting is learning to use what you were born with. Well, maybe I just wasn't born with it. I'm still five metres behind everybody. No amount of technique will make that up."

"Yeah, sure, it's easy for you kids to give up these days. In my day, I'll tell you, my coach would have whipped me for talk of giving up. Not today's kids, that's for sure. I thought we could make you into an 800-metre runner. You had some promise." He made it sound as though Noah had given up a leg, or toes, and would never be able to run again.

"Look, I'm sorry if I disappointed you. I've worked hard. And I'd still like to be in the club. That is, if Coach Buchan will have me."

"I'll tell him it's okay with me. But it's not going to be any easier there. He'll work your butt off. You think I'm a tough coach? Buchan will run you to the ground every day of the week. You'll see."

Noah dropped his eyes. Judge's disappointment wasn't making this any easier, and Noah had not expected it. On the way to the track that morning, he had even wondered if the ex-sprinter would care at all about his decision to join the distance runners. But maybe he does care about his runners, Noah thought, and he just thinks I'm lazy.

"I'm not afraid of work," Noah said. "I'm not."

"Yeah," said Judge. "Yeah. Look, you'll learn some day that you can't jump to something new because things don't pan out right away. Let's just hope you don't learn the hard way."

Noah swallowed a burning lump. He thinks I'm giving up, he thought. He turned to go, then spun around. "Anyway, thanks. Thanks for everything."

Judge adjusted his sunglasses. The mirrors were up again. "Okay. Yeah. See you around the track, Meyers." He banged his clipboard once against his right thigh and walked toward the infield, still shaking his head.

* * *

John Buchan was more relaxed than his colleague. "Sure. Be glad to have you run with us. Any time."

Noah faltered, then tried again. "But more than just run with you. I would like you to coach me. You know. Give me workouts. Stuff like that."

Buchan looked at him with a smile. "Even after that painful run in Lindsay, you still want to run distances?"

Noah shrugged. "I just think I'd be better at it."

"You could be right. You've got the stamina, determination. I'll have to talk this over with Bill Judge, though. I don't want him to think I'm stealing his athletes. But if you want distance, we'll give you distance. Come on, let's tell the others, then get warmed up."

Noah followed Buchan to the infield corner where Marc Ascott, Diane White, and three other distance runners had gathered.

"Hey, people!" he said. "Noah is going to join us for distance workouts from now on."

"All right!" said Diane, lifting her right hand for a high-five.

Marc offered his palm for a low-five. "Glad to have you," he said, grinning.

The others gathered round, echoing Diane and Marc's welcome. Buchan put down his clipboard, shed his tracksuit down to shorts and jersey, and wordlessly led the runners out on the track, jogging easily.

"We usually do about six, maybe eight laps like this," he said to Noah, who had quickly taken up the pace beside him. "Fifteen, maybe twenty minutes. Then we'll do our workout. Today, that's supposed to be four to six 800-metre intervals. Then we'll do another six to eight laps of warm-down."

Noah added up the laps mentally. Two and a half laps to a kilometre. Three kilometres of warm-up. Three kilometres of workout. Three more of warm down. Ten kilometres. In one day.

"You sure you don't want to go back to sprinting?" asked Diane. "They get to lie about the infield a lot and rest."

Buchan smiled. "Well, Noah can skip the intervals for the first two weeks."

Noah ran at Buchan's side. "Why?"

"You've got to build a base first. You've got the legs for speed now, as much as you're going to get. What you have to build is endurance. That'll only come with easy distance. You get that foundation, then we'll put you through some intervals. In the meantime, you should run every day, not just on track nights. And, of course, you'll join us for the long run on Sunday."

"Long run?"

"Sure," said Diane. "Every Sunday we do a long run, an hour to an hour and a half. Eight o'clock every Sunday morning. Rain or shine. Summer or winter."

"She's not kidding," said Buchan.

An hour and a half? Without a stop? Noah privately wondered if there was such a time as eight o'clock on his Sunday morning clock.

"Sprinters get to sleep in," he replied, "a lot."

Diane White laughed. "Distance runners," she said, "only get to go to bed earlier. They're usually so tired they can't do much else."

10

A Stolen Base

When Noah told the family that he had switched from sprinting to distance running, his uncle Max pretended he didn't understand. He sat at his favourite chair in the kitchen, tipping back on two legs, his hands folded in front of him. His glasses had coffee-grease fingerprints on the lenses. His longish, curly brown hair had not been combed. Adam sat across the table, devouring a pre-game orange. Mrs. Meyers sipped a cup of camomile tea.

"But you're a distance runner *now*," he said. "Every time you run, you run a distance. 100 metres is short, but it's a distance."

"Uncle Max! Sometimes you are so silly!"

"Relax. It's a sign that you're growing up. Impatience with others. That's why I've vowed to never grow up."

Noah grimaced. "Well, you're doing a very good job, Peter Pan."

"Oh, zingers, eh? Very good. But as a distance runner, you can now play Peter Pan and also never grow up."

"Which means?"

"Put it this way. Long distance runners don't want to carry a lot of useless weight. A good distance runner is a skinny runt. You'll never look muscle-bound like Arnold Whatzhizsnortsel."

Adam snorted. "Won't help fight off the bullies," he said.

Mrs. Meyers lifted an eyebrow. "Having trouble with bullies?"

"Nothing I can't deal with," Noah replied. Under the table, Noah shook his closed fist at Adam.

Mrs. Meyers noticed the gesture. She poured another cup of tea. "If there's a problem, you should share it with us."

"So about the running," Max interjected. "How did Bill Judge react when you told him? You have told him, I presume."

"He didn't kiss me on both cheeks and cheer, if that's what you mean," Noah said. "He hassled me a bit. More like a cold shoulder. But he's treated me like that all the time, anyway."

Mrs. Meyers smiled weakly. "Bill Judge has never been the warmest human being," she said. "When they were starting up the Clarington Vikings three years ago, some parents thought he might turn kids off."

"There's not much fooling around," Noah replied. "And he seemed to lean on me more than most."

Max brought his chair down on all four legs. "But he gets results. And one of these days, one of his runners will be a provincial champ. Like he never was."

"He almost made it. Then he quit," said Mrs. Meyers. "It was your father who got him back into track as a coach."

"How'd that happen?" asked Noah.

"That was back when we were just starting the store. A couple of people from the Oshawa Legion Track Club came in asking us to price track outfits. In the conversation, they said they were looking for a sprint coach. Your dad remembered Judge. To make a long story short, your dad called him and talked him into sharing his track knowledge by coaching. He'd been away from track for eight years."

"And the rest is history," said Max.

"Not quite, said Mrs. Meyers. "He coached for the Legion for several years. Then, three years ago, when a group was forming the Clarington Vikings, they asked him to get involved. He was living in the old town of Bowmanville by then, which is right in the centre of Clarington."

"From the sounds of the static he gave you, he hasn't changed much," said Max. "Maybe he's afraid that you're about to give up."

"But I just changed events," Noah said. "That's different than quitting."

"We all get locked into our little foibles," said Mrs. Meyers. "Sometimes our emotions are like our muscles. They get cramped up and won't work right. Maybe they just need a little massaging, too."

Adam stood up from the table, orange juice running down his chin. "Hey! Look at the time! I've got to get to my game." He grabbed his glove, then looked around, particularly at Noah.

"You coming?"

"We'll all go," said Mrs. Meyers. "That is, unless your uncle has something more important?"

Max consulted his watch. "I have a movie date at eight," he said. "I may have to leave early. But I'd love to watch your game, Tiger." He ruffled Adam's hair, grinning like an uncle.

Adam grimaced, then grinned back. "Let's go, then."

* * *

Adam's team played all of its home games on the community diamond behind the neighbourhood school. When they arrived, a few players from each team were already warming up.

"I can't get used to these kids playing baseball," Max said.

Mrs. Meyers looked at him. "It's different, isn't it?"

"Hey, yeah, when I was Adam's age, we played softball. You know, bigger ball, underhand pitching, no leadoff, closer bases."

"Well, some still do. But a lot of teams have switched to baseball. That's no wonder, what with the Blue Jays and all."

"I guess a lot of things have changed," Max said, after a pause.

The game had attracted the usual crowd: seventeen parents from both sides, an older man walking his dog, and a kindergarten-age kid with a red balloon running ahead of his young parents. Behind the backstop screen, Ian Brant slouched, his hands in his jeans' pockets. Rhonda Rogers, black lipstick and all, leaned on his shoulder.

"Hey, Meyers," said Rhonda. "Found your girlfriend, the Olympic runner?"

Noah turned for just a moment. "Why don't you two go and mutate into something useful?" he replied.

When Noah, his mother, and Max finally found a spot on the bleachers, Mrs. Meyers turned to Noah. "What was that all about?"

"Just two creeps from my class at school. I hope I don't see them in high school."

"That's the kid who chums with Neil Zeko," Max said.

"And that's Rhonda Rogers," said Mrs. Meyers. "You were in kindergarten with her, for goodness sake. Her mother told me last month that since she got remarried, Rhonda's been ... difficult."

"Looks like a lulu to me," Max said.

Noah didn't mind their looks: Rhonda's ghostly makeup, Ian's snarly coat, and in-your-face haircut. It was the way the two acted, their bullying, that he could not accept.

Adam's team dropped one run in the first inning, two more in the third, and another in the fifth. This last run came from a blooper over second base, scoring a run from second.

One of the parents began to rant at Adam's coach, waving his arms and yelling from the stands.

"What's the matter, you dumb or something? Move those fielders over. Any fool could see what was coming! Come on, wake up!" The centre fielder hung his head in embarrassment. It was his father doing the yelling.

Adam's coach caught the umpire's eye, held his hands up in the classic *T*-sign. Time out. He motioned slowly to the yelling father to meet him at the bench. Puzzled, the father reluctantly walked over. The two exchanged words quietly, with arms waving.

"I think he just got told to sit down and shut up," said Max.

"I would hope so. Last thing a coach needs is to have some hyperactive parent second-guessing him," said Mrs. Meyers. "Remember when I coached your team, Noah? Some parents — you wouldn't believe."

That was three years ago. Noah's father had been the coach at the beginning of that season. Then he got sick, and Mrs. Meyers had taken over.

It had been a good summer for Noah, at least at first. Both of his parents were at home for most of the time in the early part of the summer vacation. But his father grew tired, and slept a lot. He went from being a busy athlete involved in many sports, to a tired old man with pain in his eyes.

Noah remembered the hospital visits. He remembered the dinging of the elevator bells, the smell of meal carts in the corridors, and the mixture of antiseptic, medicine, and flowers. Even now, the word cancer would bring back those same sounds and smells.

Bottom of the seventh. Last inning. Max stayed to watch Adam's final bat.

Adam hit a grounder through first and second, and made it to first. He stole second, then third, not unusual in this league, since ten-year-old catchers cannot make a quick throw to third. With Adam on third with the tying run, and two out, Max waved his goodbye to Adam, pointing to his watch. He was already late for his date.

With the count two and two, the opposing pitcher threw a wild shot that got away from the catcher. Adam, already with a two-metre leadoff, pounced on the chance and broke for home.

The pitcher saw the steal attempt, yelled once and headed for the plate. The catcher gave a quick underhand toss, just as Adam began his slide.

"Yrrrr OUT!" growled the ump, his right thumb jerked backward.

Adam made a face, got up out of the dirt to brush himself off, and limped from the field, dejected.

He was still limping as they walked home.

"Good try," said Noah. "You mighta made it."

"Is that leg going to be okay?" asked Mrs. Meyers. "I'll clean it off when we get home."

"It's just a bit of diamond pizza," said Adam. "It's not like anybody'll have to amputate or anything."

"What did your coach say?" Noah asked.

"He was pretty mad," Adam replied. "He said if I ever tried a steal like that again, without waiting for the signal from the base coach, he'd bench me." Adam paused, grimaced once, and then grinned.

"But I'm not worried. He can't bench me," Adam continued. "He needs me at shortstop. Besides, how do I ever get better at stealing bases if I don't practise?"

11

A Long Sunday Run

Noah's alarm rang at seven o'clock on Sunday.
A month before, when he was a sprinter, seven o'clock did not exist on Sunday mornings. Now sleepy-eyed, Noah groped for the clock, silencing it on the third swipe. Slowly, still under the covers, he stretched, his taut muscles warming slowly to the day. He swung his feet to the floor.

In the kitchen, he glided barefoot in pyjamas from pantry to toaster. One, no, two pieces of toast, with strawberry jam, and orange juice.

Once upon a time, Noah could not have imagined running for ninety minutes, especially before breakfast. The first time he went on the Sunday morning long run with the distance group, he had risen early and eaten his regular breakfast: a bowl of cereal, a banana, orange juice, and a couple of pieces of toast. Running did burn off energy, he reasoned.

Mistake. BIG mistake.

Stomach cramps had caught him that day after forty minutes. The group then spent much of their running time looking for an open service station with a rest room.

From then on, Noah had limited his pre-run snack to a couple of pieces of toast. Breakfast, a big breakfast, would come after the run. By then he would need food to replace the energy burned up in the long jog.

Buchan had been amused, but instructive. "About sixty calories to a kilometre," he said. "A thousand calories on a ninety-minute run. Simple arithmetic. But after the run, not before."

By 7:50 a.m., Noah was waiting in the driveway. Slowly, he performed a series of easy stretches. One, standing at an angle against the wall with legs straight, for the calves; another leaning forward for Achilles tendons; and a third with one leg raised on the railing, leaning forward until his forehead touched his knee. He also did a few ankle rotations.

At exactly 8:02, six people jogged down the middle of the residential street, moving easily, chatting happily. What was it his father used to say? Like magpies. Funny, thought Noah, as he watched the joggers approach, how, after two years, memories of his father would come curving through in happy moments.

The group included Buchan, of course, as well as Marc Ascott and Diane White. Three other distance runners, two from the club and one older runner Noah had met somewhere before, were also jogging.

"Got the sleep out of your eyes?" Buchan asked as they approached. Noah jogged down the driveway, joining the group before they would have to slow for him.

"I'll just sleep through this run, thanks. It's easier that way," he replied. "If I wake up I'll have to work at it."

"Well, wake me when this is over," said one guy, in his mid-teens. "But this sure ain't my idea of a dream."

"Whatever."

Buchan introduced the other two runners, then said, "And this old guy here is Harvey Thomson." He gestured to the older runner, in his late thirties or early forties. "He's planning to run a marathon next month and he needs all the company for long runs he can find."

The man smiled and greeted Noah. "I knew your dad," he said, as they turned the corner at the end of his street. "Your uncle still running that store? What's it called, Fast Finish?"

Lots of people had known his dad. Even two years after the funeral people still would say that, and still Noah did not know how to reply.

"Him and my mom," he mumbled.

"Your dad would've liked this," the man continued, as though it should mean something. "He was a pretty good runner, you know."

Noah hadn't known. Or if he had, his memory of that part of his father had got buried in the memories of illness, treatment, and more illness that had gone on for what seemed forever.

Buchan laughed. "'Pretty good' means he used to beat Harvey all the time."

Harvey said, "Well, I don't remember seeing you beat him either, John."

"I had a fifteen-year head start on him," said Buchan. "Besides, we didn't race as much then."

"I didn't know you ran with him," said Noah. "I didn't even know he ran much."

"We ran for fun, back then," Buchan replied. "Your dad ran mostly to keep in shape for squash and tennis. But when he did race, he was deadly."

Noah shifted to the far side of the pack, away from the marathon runner. "Well, I still think we're all crazy. Real people are sleeping in. Right this instant," he complained.

Buchan laughed, "If you think this is crazy, being out here in early September weather with the sun shining — well, you just wait until we're out here in the wind and the snow and the rain and the freezing and the … "

"Huh?" snorted Marc Ascott, in mock alarm. "Nobody ever told me about that part."

"I'll sleep through that, too," said Noah. "Even on my feet."

They jogged slowly, bobbing along at about five minutes a kilometre. No one breathed deeply; no one showed discomfort. At first, Noah was convinced that he could keep up such a pace all day. He had told Buchan as much on his first long run.

"Don't you believe it," he said. "This seems easy for the first hour. Maybe two. But at five minutes a kilometre, you'd finish a marathon in three and a half hours."

"That's not very fast."

"No, it's not fast. An hour and fifteen minutes slower than world class for men, an hour slower than world class for women. But beyond the thirty-two kilometre mark, strange things happen to your body. Your body stores only enough energy to last thirty-two kilometres. After that, you hit the wall. You run like you're stuck in molasses."

"It hurts?"

"Oh, sure. Nothing you can't plug through. But often it takes people an hour to push through these last ten kilometres. Many just don't finish. You need lots of endurance training, lots of long runs, like this one, even to run distances from one kilometre and up."

"Like the bear on the back?"

"Well, no. You go out too fast in the 1500-metre race, for instance, and after two laps you will start to go into oxygen debt. Your legs begin to feel like tree stumps. Even your arms get heavy. The last lap and three quarters are going to be tough. That's the bear on the back. To overcome that, you train with faster intervals. To prepare for the marathon, to push the wall back, you train with long, slow runs, building endurance. Then you work on speed."

At the eleven kilometre mark they reached the foot of Trull's Road Mountain.

"We're goin' up that?" asked Marc. "That's straight up."

Trull's Road Mountain was really just a steep hill marking what ten thousand years ago had been the north shore of Lake Ontario. To runners standing at the bottom, it looked like a mountain.

"Man, I'll need climbing gear to go up that," said the older runner. "If we get halfway up that and stop, we'll fall off."

"No one told me we were going this route this morning," said Marc. "If I'da known, I'da had the flu."

The hill rose slowly from a little dip, the slope gentle at first. Lifting his eyes to the top, Noah could not see the crest of the hill, but knew it would be about 800 metres away.

After 200 metres, the slope steepened. The runners focused on the job at hand, pushing with each footstep, breathing in shorter gasps. Nobody talked. Their legs, tensed to the job, soon showed fatigue.

"And ... to ... think," said Buchan, sucking in air between words and breaking the silence, "that I ... do this ... for ... fun."

"Let's get this over quicker," Diane White said at about the halfway mark. "Race you to the top!"

Noah looked at her for signs of a foaming mouth. "You're crazy."

Diane shrugged. "Stay back here if you wish," she said, "but I'm going to get this over." She surged ahead, her long legs stretching the distance between them by one, two, three metres and counting.

Noah shrugged again, and looked back at Buchan. Marc and the other guys seemed to be happy where they were.

"We'll see," he said to himself. Where the hill became steeper, he surged after Diane, aiming at her heels six metres ahead. This is why Diane is so good, he thought. She's willing to push hard when others are content to sit back and coast. That's not a bad philosophy, he told himself.

After ten strides, Noah's legs tightened up. This was crazy, he told himself; doing hill surges on a twenty-kilometre run.

Then he noticed that Diane was still only six metres ahead. Which meant ...

"Catch 'er, Noah," a voice urged. Buchan, perhaps.

Noah pushed harder, right where the hill climbed steepest. Diane was six, then five metres ahead, then four.

The slope eased off, the last 200 metres to the top levelling slowly. Three metres, two metres. Noah's eyes focused on Diane's back, right between her shoulder blades. One metre, then he was even with her. His lungs hurt. One more stride. Noah pushed until Diane fell back at his left elbow. They were nearing the top now, one telephone pole length to go.

Zwish! Noah was still pumping hard when Diane pushed by again on his right side. Before he could respond, she had crested the hill and began to ease her pace.

"Wow!" was all Diane could say between gasps as they eased to a jog. "You're picking ... up some good ... speed."

Noah gulped air. "Not ... good ... enough."

Buchan chided them both with a chuckle when the other runners caught them. "You like to run with a bear on your back, eh? You're going to pay for this," he said. "Only eight more kilometres to go. Do you think you can behave the rest of the way?"

Noah rolled his eyes, his chest heaving as he drank in air. "You can count on me."

"Just remember: speed is for the track. And for races. This long run is for endurance only. So we don't add anything with speed bursts. Except," he smiled. "Fun."

Noah and Diane were still gulping in air, trying to recover. And, Noah thought, it *was* fun.

12

Adam's Tantrum

It was half-past five on a mid-September evening, thirty minutes before game time. Adam Meyers sat on the family room floor, his face twisted, his baseball cap on sideways, his team uniform looking on him as though it belonged to someone else. He tossed his baseball at a certain spot on the floor in front of his knee, caught the bounce and then repeated the throw. Thump.

"If he puts me in left field again." Thump. "I won't play," he said. Thump. Thump.

"You don't mean that," said Mrs. Meyers. It was the type of thing most mothers would say.

"I mean it. I really mean it. I'm not standing out there doing nothing all night. It's not as though I haven't played okay. At least he could put me where I want to be." Thump. Thump. THUMP.

Max, who had joined the family for dinner for the third time in a week, sipped at his coffee. "Yeah, but your coach has a team to run. Maybe he's figured out what's best for the team."

Adam wasn't convinced. "Yeah, sure." Thump. THUMP. Thump.

"It's getting close to game time," Mrs. Meyers said. "We should get going."

"Come on, let's motor, buddy," Max added.

Adam pulled away from the attempt to tousle his hair. "I'm nobody's buddy," he retorted.

Just then, Noah came in. He had been reading a book in his room: *Stairway to the Olympics.*

"Adam, you look as though you've been benched," he said.

Thump. Thump. THUMP.

"Almost ..." Thump. "As bad."

"The coach put him in left field last game. He didn't touch the ball all night," Max said, turning to Noah.

"That must've been disappointing," Noah replied.

"Yeah. Right."

"But you hit all right, didn't you? Sorry I missed that game last night. You know. Track. But I've done my workout for today. I'm ready and rarin' to go."

"If he puts me in left field there won't be anything to see." Thump. "I'm going ... " Thump. " ... home." THUMP.

Mrs. Meyers tidied some papers on her roll-top desk. "Well, we won't know until we get there, will we? And," she added, "it is time to go. So make up your mind. Are you going or not?"

Thump. THUMP. "I'll go." Thump. "But if he puts me in left field, I'm gone." Thump. Thump.

Noah exchanged glances with his mother and Max.

* * *

The first five innings of Adam's game went smoothly. Adam, despite his fears, played shortstop. He stole two bases, including a run. In the fourth inning he batted in the second run to give his team a one-run lead.

"Way to go, Adam!" Noah liked to yell, even though he could see it embarrassed his little brother.

Noah, his mother, and Max sat behind Adam's team's bench. They watched the coach approach Adam as he started to take to the field for the sixth inning.

"Meyers," said the coach. "You take left field. Zwartzentruber's going in for shortstop."

"Left field?" queried Adam, his eyes shifting to his mother for an instant. "Left field?"

"Yeah. You got the leg speed we need. You also back up plays pretty good. Let's get a move on."

Adam's face fell. His chin dropped. He looked at the ground, kicked once, twice. "I ain't playing left field," he said.

The coach turned, slowly. "Meyers. You in or out?"

Adam kicked once more at the ground. "Ain't playin' left field." Kick, kick.

"Okay, have it your way. Take the bench. Kelly, you take left field. Zwartzentruber, shortstop. Let's hustle, guys."

Adam stood, stunned, his glove hanging loosely from his left hand. "I want to play short," he said. The coach had turned and moved on to other decisions.

His face contorted with rage, Adam kicked at the wire mesh fence of the dugout. The fence shuddered, then swayed along its whole length.

"Meyers," said the coach. "Bench! Now!"

Adam kicked once more at the protective fencing and stormed past the dugout. "Stuff your stupid bench!" he said. As he tried to squeeze by, the coach held out his arm to bar the way.

"Stay on the bench, and you're still part of this team," he said. "Leave now, and you're not. We need your bat for the playoffs."

Adam twisted away. "Shove your bat," he said. He pushed his way past the bleachers, avoiding his mother's eyes.

"Shove your stupid playoffs!" He yelled as he headed off across the park.

Mrs. Meyers moved to follow him. Max held her sleeve for a moment. "Not now," he said. "Give him some space. I'll talk to him."

"He can't act like that. It's embarrassing! I just won't tolerate that kind of behaviour," Mrs. Meyers said.

Max smiled. "Neither would his father, you know that. But he's got a lot of rage built up. It's got to come out somewhere."

"Rage? We can't excuse everything because his father died, can we?" said Mrs. Meyers. "Besides, it's been two years."

"It's been two years and you've just started to notice the rest of the world yourself," said Max. "The kid has no idea why he's angry. Is it at his father for dying? At you for grieving? I don't know. Maybe he's angry at me, for being a corny uncle."

Noah followed them to the parking lot, where they found Adam, who sat in the back seat all the way home, his arms folded across his chest in defiance. He said nothing.

13

A Track Race

A few days later, Buchan limped across the infield toward Noah.

"Hi, kid! Feeling spiffy and ready to go?"

Noah smiled. "I can give it a try. Whatever. What's with the limp? Age catching up?"

Buchan grinned. "I don't know. Runner's knee. Tendinitis, likely. Sometimes it feels just like a red hot needle in the side of my knee. It's bothered me ever since our long run on Sunday."

Marc looked up from where he was tying his laces on the ground beside Noah. "First your hair falls out, now your joints are creaking. Better switch to soft food next, old fella."

Buchan laughed. "Better to wear out running marathons than to rust out from lack of use," he said, running a teasing hand through Marc's dark hair. "I've been tracking your race times, remember."

Turning to Noah, he opened his clipboard. "See, Meyers, I bought this clipboard so I could look like a real coach. And what it says right here is that you've been working out with the distance runners for eight weeks now."

"Time flies when you're having fun," Noah retorted.

"Right. A quick tongue, too. Anyway, I figure you're about ready to find out how fit you are. Thursday night we're going to Toronto for an all-comers' meet at York University. I think you're ready for a try at the 3000-metre."

"What's that in real distance?"

"Seven and a half laps. Three kilometres."

"Racing?"

"The all-comers' meet lets you pick out which heat you want to run. There's nothing at stake. It's more like a time trial. Except, of course, you have a bit of competition, to keep you honest, and a real stop watch."

Noah shrugged, trying to hide his excitement. "I'm game. What sort of time should I be aiming at?"

Buchan referred to his clipboard. "You're not ready for a world record. Yet. I figure you should be able to go under eleven and a half minutes, for sure. Eleven would impress me a lot, ten and a half would blow just about everybody away, I think."

Later, Noah watched while Buchan limped across to the infield bench while Marc, Diane and others ran their warm-up routine. For the first time since they met, Buchan looked like the grandfather he was.

* * *

The track facility at York University had a reputation as the best in the province. Indoors, it boasted a banked 200-metre track and a 100-metre straight sprint track. All these were ideal for winter workouts.

But it was not winter. Noah and the visiting Vikings used the indoor facility only for the dressing rooms. Then they headed outdoors.

The outdoor track looked bigger than the 400-metre track at home. Buchan assured them it was not. The outdoor and indoor tracks were part of a sports complex that included a professional-level tennis court.

Buchan gave them a quick tour. "I've already registered everybody in their events. Just to keep you all on track and on time, I've prepared a copy for each of you." He handed everyone a list of events. "Just remember that the event times are estimates. Start your warm-up twenty minutes before the event time, and keep it easy, slow. Half a dozen 100-metre strides about ten minutes before your event would be good. But try to keep an eye on where we are on the list. They get ahead of schedule sometimes. You don't want to miss your event. That happened once to American sprinters in an Olympic final. On the other hand, if they're running late you don't want to stay warmed up for an hour. You'll be too pooped to participate."

Noah looked at the sheet. The 3000 was set for seven o'clock. Half an hour.

Buchan limped over. "Noah, my boy," he said. "I had hoped there would be two heats in the 3000. That way we could've put you in the slower one. That'd be enough challenge for the first time. But they had only eight entries tonight, so they're running them all together. That means there's going to be some pretty fast people out there. Don't get sucked into going out with the leaders. You'll not enjoy the last five laps if you do."

"Five laps? It's only seven."

"Seven and a half. You'd likely stick with the leaders for about two laps. They'll be running close to your best 800-metre time. From then on you'd be sucking air and in deep oxygen debt. You'd likely have to drop out. Just run the first lap without stress and let it go from there. Good luck."

"Thanks."

By the time he got to the start line, Noah felt he needed more than luck.

The other seven people who lined up with him included two women from the York track team; an eleven-year-old boy who kept bouncing up and down like Tigger from Winnie-the-Pooh; a grey-haired guy around Buchan's age; an older woman, about sixty, with white hair, dressed in the maroon colours of the Longboat running club; and two men, in their early forties, sporting green and maroon.

They're about the same age as my father would have been, Noah thought.

"Your first?" the white-haired woman said to Noah as they shook their muscles loose at the start line.

"I've done one road race," he answered.

"Just don't overdo the first lap. Those two," she pointed to the two university track team members, "are going to go out fast and stay fast. Don't get sucked in. Unless you want to run it in 9:30 or so. The bear will get on your back soon enough."

Noah said thanks just as the starter raised her arm.

"Mark!" she yelled.

The runners toed the line, coiled like steel springs.

BANG!

At the sound, they were off, jostling for position. Noah tried to behave himself, and fall in behind the others. His plan had been to stay behind everyone for the first lap, and then see how things felt.

His plan proved impossible from the first stride. For one thing, the oldest male runner had the same idea. For the first dozen strides he kept motioning for Noah to go ahead.

Finally, Noah gave up and moved forward. That put him in seventh place — not last, second last.

The two university runners had easily taken the lead, gliding smoothly around the top of the track. The blond led easily, her long legs eating distance in a tireless stride. Behind her, the brunette hung on as though it were no effort. As they turned down the first back straight, Tigger, bouncing along with arms and legs flailing, moved with them.

Noah moved around the older woman runner, who offered a corner of a smile but no words. Sixth place. But Noah was moving easily. He felt strength in his legs and lungs.

On the back straight he pulled in behind the two runners in their forties. He was about to move around them, when one spoke:

"Hey, take it easy. There's lots of time."

"Lookit that kid, would you?" said the other man. Ahead, Tigger had taken second place, flailing along between the two university women as they passed the 400-metre mark.

"Yeah, but now watch him fade," replied the other.

Sure enough, as they continued down the back straight, the leaders started around the second bend. Halfway around, Tigger began to flounder, his smooth easy stride now jerky, like a puppet with tangled strings. The number two runner, silky smooth, passed him as they turned toward the front straight.

"Told ya," said a voice behind Noah.

" ... 1:23, 1:24, 1:25 ... " An official with a stopwatch called out the time as they completed the first lap. One minute, twenty-three seconds.

"That's a 10:30 pace," predicted one of the experienced runners, dressed in green, glancing at this watch. "Right on target."

Ten minutes and thirty seconds! Noah couldn't believe what he'd heard. He was a minute ahead of target. And he knew he could run like this forever.

Halfway through the second lap they passed Tigger. Now in fifth place, Noah began to work his arms. Then the two men moved ahead. One second Noah was with them, and the next moment he trailed by a few metres. He pushed harder and caught them again. Now, as they rounded the last curve of lap two, he was working hard for the first time.

" ... 2:47, 2:48 ... "

Noah ran in a pack of three with two master runners. The one in green took the lead, with Noah and the maroon runner one second back. Up front, by 100 metres, the blond university runner had opened up a ten-metre lead on her teammate. As Noah finished lap two, the lead runners were already entering the back straight.

On the third lap, Noah and his maroon partner passed the guy in green, leading him by one second. Fourth place.

" ... 4:13, 4:14, 4:15 ... "

He was now running beside the runner in the maroon top. For one strange moment, Noah realized he was tied for third place. A distant third, of course, but third nevertheless.

"Keep it up, Meyers! Keep it up! Looking good. Looking good!" Buchan yelled from the side of the track, slapping his clipboard on his hip. "Stay with them!"

In lap four, Noah felt his lungs begin to burn. His arms became lead weights. Although he sensed he was still running with the same power and speed, he began to fall behind. One stride, then two. Fifth place.

" ... 5:40, 5:41, 5:42 ... "

The maroon runner was half a dozen paces ahead. The man in green was two seconds ahead. Noah thought he could catch them, but it no longer seemed so important.

" ... 7:10, 7:11, 7:12 ... "

By the end of lap five, the times no longer had meaning. Suddenly, beside Noah, was the Longboat runner he'd spoken to at the start line.

"You're doing great, kid," she said. "Stay with me. We'll help each other the rest of the way." Noah could only nod, gasping for air, marvelling that this woman, older than his mother, a grandmother perhaps, could run this fast, and still talk.

The maroon and green runners were now almost a quarter lap ahead, moving down the back straight as Noah turned into the top curve.

Noah could not keep up with the woman. Down the back straight he watched her pull away. By the end of the lap he was forty metres back. Sixth place.

" … 8:43, 8:44 … "

Lap six. One and a half more to go. Each step required Noah to pull hard in an all-out sprint. But he didn't have any speed left. No! he told himself. He'd not let thoughts of quitting begin.

Behind him he could hear footsteps, laboured breathing. The runner Noah estimated to be about Buchan's age, fiftyish, pulled up beside him. His breath came in deep gasps. He didn't try to speak. He edged ahead, leaving Noah in seventh place.

Somewhere on the last bend of lap seven even the older man pulled ahead, five, seven, nine, twelve, thirteen metres. The two university women passed Noah again running flat out in their finishing kick, now a full lap ahead.

" … 9:31, 9:32 … "

Noah was now halfway round the sixth lap. A second official stood by the track ringing a large hand bell.

CLANG! CLANG! CLANG!

"One lap, one lap, one lap!"

The bell lap. Once more around the track. Now ten seconds behind the older runner, Noah glanced ahead. In front of him, Tigger trudged along. But how? he wondered. He had passed that kid years ago, back in, what? Lap two?

Then Noah realized what had happened. There was Tigger, forty metres ahead, with one lap to go. He could lap him!

Noah surged forward, all his effort in an even stride. One of the York University runners, now finished, had turned and was jogging back along the inside of the track. She flashed Noah a wide smile.

"Great run! Go get 'em! You're looking good!" she said.

Then, as Noah passed, she raised her hand for a high-five. Noah smacked the hand as he went by, all muscles tensed and working, his mind fixed tightly on the back of Tigger's shirt.

Five, four, three, two, one metre to go. Then he was around him. He had been lapped by the leaders, but in turn he had lapped one runner.

Around the last bend Noah caught another runner and kicked around him, his lungs burning but legs flying. Sixth.

On the last straight he could see the grey-haired woman in the Longboat colours, still running strongly but coming back nevertheless. Closer, closer, closer.

" ... 10:55, 10:56 ... "

The race was over. Ten minutes and fifty-six seconds! Sixth place.

Noah had broken eleven minutes. The woman with the Longboat colours had finished in 10:52: four seconds, maybe fifteen metres ahead. Behind him by four strides, another man pounded across the finish line. But Noah had finished in sixth place! And he had lapped Tigger the kid.

What had Buchan said? Noah wondered. That he could run the race in under eleven minutes? And he had.

Noah was still sucking air into his lungs, his hands on the back of his hips, when his teammates caught him on the track.

"Great run, Noah!"

"Way to pop! You really put on a surge that last lap and a half."

Buchan snapped the clasp on his clipboard. "You're a natural," he said. "A little more racing experience and you're going to be bringing home some hardware. Ten minutes and fifty-six seconds! Wow!"

On the trip home in the van, Buchan suggested they attend a 1500-metre race the next weekend. Noah felt too elated to question it. Half the length of the 3000, the 1500-metre run should be simple, he thought.

Little did he know.

14

Picking Up the Pieces

The family conference was filled with angry silences. Adam sat on the family room floor by the wood stove staring at the carpet. Noah lounged in his favourite chair, the recliner. Mrs. Meyers sat upright on the wooden swivel chair at her desk. Max stood on the bottom step of the half flight of stairs leading to the kitchen, rocking back and forth on his toes.

"So what's the next step?" asked Max.

"Step? There is no step. I quit the team last week. I thought that was pretty clear." Adam sounded defiant, but Noah thought his eyes did not look so sure.

Mrs. Meyers leaned forward in her chair. "Yes, you did quit the team. And if you wish, you can just leave it at that. And you can sit here and play computer games and feel sorry for yourself, too."

"I'm not feeling sorry for myself."

In the silence that followed, a trapped fly buzzed between the window panes.

"Can I do anything to help?" Noah asked, finally.

Adam gestured to his mother and Max. "Yeah. Tell these two to leave me alone."

"I'm just here as a scratching post," said Max.

"Using me as a punching bag," retorted Adam.

"Whatever. You've dug yourself into a hole. You've poured in a gallon of self-pity. And now you're starting to wallow in it," Max said.

"Am not!"

"Look. You didn't act like a team player. The coach can't let you back on the team now for any reason. Still, you do owe him and the team an apology. Whether you give him one or not is up to you," Max continued.

"You can't tell me what to do! You're not my father!"

Mrs. Meyers and Max exchanged glances.

"No. I'm your uncle. I care about you. I would like to help you."

"Then butt out."

Mrs. Meyers held up her right index finger. "Max is only trying … "

"Then tell him to stop trying!" Adam started to sob.

"Trying to hurt me, or your mother, or Noah, is not going to bring your father back. Throwing tantrums or baseball bats and quitting the team isn't going to help either," said Max, gently.

Adam was now sobbing openly. "I didn't want to quit! I didn't want him to let me quit!"

Mrs. Meyers tried to explain. "But the coach doesn't have time for that. He has a whole team to deal with. And when you let your anger go, you have to know that you can't get it back again. You have to live with the consequences."

"I just want to play."

Max headed for the kitchen with his empty coffee mug. "I can phone the coach and ask … "

 Mrs. Meyers held up a hand. "With respect, Max, this is really Adam's problem. He has to deal with it."

"But you heard him. He didn't really mean it."

Mrs. Meyers shook her head, and waved Max to the kitchen. "The point is, Adam, that some things you say and do can't be taken back. You quit the team. It has to be you who apologizes to the coach. And I don't think you should expect him to let you back on the team."

"Then why apologize?" asked Adam, with a sniffle.

His mother met his stare. "You know the answer to that."

"What would Dad have made me do?"

"You know the answer to that, too. We all loved your dad, and we miss him. Every day. Even after almost two years, it hurts. I think of him often." Her voice quavered.

"But … "

"Listen. Even if your dad were alive now, you wouldn't do everything he wanted. You would be arguing, fighting, working out compromises. Now you've got that all mixed up with your anger and grief. That'll only hurt you."

Adam tossed a baseball from one bare hand to another. Hard. "I just couldn't help it. I just burst all at once!" Another small tear trickled down his cheek.

"I know I wasn't much help after your father died," said Mrs. Meyers. "And there are no shortcuts through grieving. Sometimes it gets all mixed up with anger."

"Anger?"

"It happened to me."

"Mom? You?" asked Noah.

"I still wake up at night and my throat aches," she said. "The worst time was two months after your dad died. The year before, he had made arrangements to have the leaky roof fixed. He either didn't tell me, or I forgot. So, anyway, one day, out of the blue, a truck and work crew arrived and began ripping the old shingles off our roof."

"I remember that. You were really mad that day," exclaimed Noah.

"Was I ever. I ordered them off the property, and told them to get lost. All of my pain and anger and grief came pouring out on this bunch of workers who were just trying to do their job. I ordered them to stop and they did. But first they had ripped most of the old shingles off the roof."

"What did you do?" Adam asked.

"I let out a lot of anger at people who didn't deserve it. And after the anger, I cried, and cried. Strangely enough, that helped a lot."

"Yeah," said Adam. "But what did you do about the shingle guys?"

"What do you think I did?"

Adam looked down at the baseball in his hand. "Apologize?" he asked.

"I had to get the company to come back and finish the roof. We'd have been in a fine fix the next time it rained," Mrs. Meyers admitted.

Adam said nothing. He buried his head in his mother's shoulder and cried. Mrs. Meyers reached out and pulled Noah toward her, too. The three embraced in a family hug. After a few moments, Noah lifted his head and met his mother's gaze.

"It's two years," he said. "How long will it be before we stop missing him so much?"

A tear trickled down his mother's cheek. "When we lose someone we love very much, the hurting never stops. We'll think about your father for the rest of our lives. Maybe we'll just get better at handling it so we don't damage ourselves in the process," she said.

Noah had been surprised by his mother's story of the roof. He realized then that grief and anger could make even adults do things to harm themselves. Adam's quitting the team hadn't hurt the coach or the team. It was Adam who suffered by not playing a game he dearly loved. Noah tried to think of anything that could trigger enough anger to make him quit running. He couldn't think of a thing.

Finally, Adam straightened his shoulders. He sniffed once, and wiped away a tear with the back of his hand.

"Guess I kinda blew it though, eh? The coach's never going to let me back on the team."

"Would you? You let him down. An apology isn't something that lets you get what you want. An apology is for someone you've hurt, needlessly. You should just say you're sorry. No strings," Mrs. Meyers advised. "It might take until next year to start again."

Adam slammed the baseball into his bare left hand.

"I guess I've got a leaky roof, eh?" he sniffed.

Mrs. Meyers smiled at both of her sons, and gave Adam a hug. "You might want to fix it before it rains," she said.

15

The 1500

Winter in Canada consists of snow, ice, slush and rain. This weather gives birth to hockey. Arenas fill with armour-plated players. Slapshots echo off boards. Pucks ping off goal posts. Players slap sticks on the ice, yell for passes.

Runners don't do any of that.

For runners, winter days mean wet feet and frostbite, running noses and chest colds, balaclavas and toques.

Noah Meyers and the other members of the Clarington Vikings considered themselves lucky. Clarington and the city of Oshawa bordered each other, and the two communities shared many facilities. In the worst weather, the club took their workouts indoors to the Oshawa Civic Dome.

There, on a 225-metre indoor track around a triple tennis court, under a huge, fabric, air-supported dome, they logged their warm-up laps, their interval laps and warm-down routine.

And they counted the days until spring.

When the first of May arrived, Noah Meyers had almost competed grade nine. He was fourteen years old. He had been running for almost a year. He was ready to race.

* * *

Noah Meyers fidgeted at the side of the track at York University. He sat with his legs straight out in front of him. He jiggled them so his knees rose and fell, rose and fell, his hamstring muscles slapping alternately on the grass.

Buchan approached, his gait awkward with a stiff-legged limp.

"Nervous?" he asked, smiling.

Noah looked up. "I'd rather catch a massasauga rattlesnake with my bare hands," he replied, smiling.

"Sure. Look. We've been over it before. You've been running a year now. Almost. You've stuck to your workouts. You've been out for the long Sunday runs almost every Sunday. You've worked hard all winter."

Noah looked up and winked at his coach. "I got in more long runs than you did this winter," he replied, teasing.

Buchan smiled. "I'll get back at it. I'm having some tests done on this leg of mine." He slapped his leg with the clipboard. "When I get that fixed up I'll be running your butt off again."

"I bet you will."

"Just remember, Noah. This 1500-metre race will be the fastest you've ever run. Don't try to lead. But don't fall too far back, either. There's nobody in this race you can't keep up with, so don't let them psyche you out."

Yeah, right, thought Noah.

"And remember: the top three go to the provincial finals next month." He turned to look at Marc. "Now, Mr. Ascott, if you don't make the top three you won't get another chance. Not in this age category. But you, young Meyers. You don't have to win. You're only fourteen, so you will be back next year as a midget. You don't want to do anything today that will hurt your career."

"Career? Yeah, I'm just waiting for those endorsements."

Buchan grinned. "This is a race of control. Stay with the leaders. There's nobody there who can out-kick you on the final 200, Meyers. But you'll never know what you can do until you get there. Those few weeks you worked with Bill Judge and the sprinters will pay dividends. That final half lap always comes down to a sprint." Buchan tapped him on the shoulder with the clipboard. "Go for it."

Twelve runners lined up their toes at the start: Noah Meyers, Marc Ascott and ten others. They faced almost four times around the track: 1500 metres. The metric mile. Noah's mouth was dry.

"MARK!"

The gun was up. The runners tensed.

BANG!

They were off. Nervous tension gave Noah Meyers a burst of energy. He darted forward, quickly slipping into the lead.

The 1500-metre race starts on the beginning of the back straight on a standard 400-metre track. Runners make three and three-quarter laps.

At the 100-metre mark, with three and a half laps to go, Noah led, his stride confident, his hair bobbing up and down.

Buchan waited at the top of the first turn. He gave Noah a quick thumbs-up, followed by a slight pushing gesture with both hands. Take it easy, he was saying. Take it easy.

Noah eased off on the next turn. One, two, three, four, five runners went by him at the top of the second lap. Black, Green, Red, Maroon, Noah thought to himself, naming the players after the colours they wore.

A race official stood at the 300-metre mark, stopwatch in hand. " ... fifty-one, fifty-two, fifty-three, fifty-four ... " he called out.

Three laps to go. Running fifth was Marc Ascott, his long stride effortless. One second back, in sixth place, was Noah Meyers. The work had not yet begun.

A year ago, Noah would not have dared to run in the same race as Marc. Now here they were, friends, two strides and one second apart — four, maybe five metres, which Noah knew he could close any time. But how would he feel two laps later? he worried.

During lap two, the runner in black lengthened his lead. Two steps behind him, Green ran strong and relaxed. The runner in the red top sucked air another fifteen metres back, with Maroon twenty metres farther back still and already showing signs of struggle.

But Marc and Noah were running stride for stride, three seconds behind Maroon, still fifth and sixth. Noah could hear other runners behind him, grunting, breathing hard. But they were invisible. Only if they passed him would they enter Noah's world, which focused on the ribbons of track in front.

" … 2:04, 2:05, 2:06 … "

Two laps down. Still running sixth.

For the first time, Noah felt fatigue. His legs had become heavier, pumping his arms required effort. He worked down the back straight, his breath now coming in deep gasps. A small pain started in his lungs and spread deeply.

He started into the bottom corner. Buchan and other Vikings were jumping up and down. He could not hear their screams, but he caught Buchan's upraised thumb. Okay, okay, okay, it said. And then Noah realized he was in fifth place. Marc had fallen back. One, two, three paces? Noah wondered. Unless Marc passed him again, Noah would never know.

Now the race took on a new shape. The runner in black, having soared to the early lead, began to tighten up and fall back. Green now took over the lead, still striding easily, relaxed.

Noah worked hard, his chest hurting as if there wasn't enough air in the whole world. Would this ever end? he asked himself. If only it were over now.

But then, unexpectedly, Noah found other runners coming back to him. Red, then Black, who had been the leader, were struggling, their muscles tightening. They were paying the price for early speed.

" … 3:24, 3:25, 3:26 … "

Suddenly, a race official rang the bell signalling the final lap. One lap to go, Noah murmured to himself. One lap to go.

Noah could see the two runners ahead of him: Green, with a twenty-metre lead, and Black. Noah could feel himself gaining until just into the bell lap, he was running third! He could qualify for the provincials, he told himself.

Noah surged around the top bend. Starting down the back straight he eased around the runner in black.

Second place. Only Green still ahead, Noah thought.

At his side, he could hear another runner panting, pulling closer from behind. On the last bend, out of the corner of his right eye, Marc Ascott edged up beside him, then smoothly, in two giant strides, glided by him on the right.

Behind him, Noah could hear the grunts of another runner. Someone was challenging him for third place.

Noah pushed ahead, forgot the pain, thankful for the work he had done the year before with the sprinters. Third place was now down to a sprint of 100 metres — down to one fast finish.

With hurting legs and red hot lungs, Noah pumped his arms, turning now into a sprinters' stride. They were heavy, as though he carried weights in them. Push, push, push, Noah told himself.

Marc was far past him now, five metres out. Nothing Noah could do would close that gap.

" … 4:29, 4:30 … " The timer called out Green's winning time.

" … 4:31, 4:32, 4:33 … "

Marc had beaten Noah with a time of four minutes and thirty-three seconds.

" … 4:34, 4:35, 4:36, 4:37 … "

Noah crossed the finish line. Third place! Four minutes and thirty-seven seconds. The provincial finals!

Three strides past the finish line Noah pulled to a stop and stepped off the track. Hands on his knees, he gasped for air.

Then Marc was in front of him. They exchanged high-fives, shouting and jumping together. They had both qualified for the finals.

Buchan limped up, let loose a wild whoop and tossed his clipboard into the air. "Great race," he said, "Both of you. You were at your best."

On the track, the runner in black who had led so easily for two laps now plodded over the finish line. His stride was defeated, his face contorted with fatigue.

One by one, other runners crossed the finish line. For many, just finishing was a triumph, to run faster than ever before and to set a personal best. For those whose dream of winning was unrealistic, it was a time of pain and disappointment.

But Noah and Marc savoured the moment, and congratulated the runner in green.

"We've got three weeks to the provincial finals," Marc said later, during their post-race warm-down. "Three weeks to find three seconds to beat Green."

"Seven seconds for some of us," Noah said.

"His name's actually Jamie Green," Buchan said. "He runs unattached — not with any club — and he always wears that colour.

"Wonder why?" Marc said.

"Seven seconds," Noah repeated. "Seven seconds."

With the race fatigue still clawing at his lungs, Noah wondered if he could ever find those seven seconds. He would have to. But he knew that Marc Ascott would find them, too. And he could never beat Marc.

16

The Left Fielder

Two days later, Adam stood in the family room of the Meyers' home, dressed in his full team colours. Now eleven, he looked forward to another season of baseball.

"You make the team?" Noah asked. That morning, Adam had attended the final try-out session for the town rep team. He sat at the desk in the family room, playing a computer baseball game. He punched a key and heard the crack of a bat.

"Yeah. Remember last fall when I quit before playoffs? I'm sure glad now I went to the coach to apologize." Click! Crack! Cheers from the electronic crowd.

"Did you make the team?"

"They posted the team after practice today."

"Did ... you ... make ... the ... team?" Noah repeated, a little louder, a little slower.

"Yeah. Guess what position?"

"Way to go, little brother." Noah stood and offered a high-five.

"Wonderful. Now guess what position."

"Shortstop?"

"You're not gonna believe this."

"Not shortstop?"

Adam looked up from the game.

"Left field," he said. "Me. Left field. I cannot quite believe it."

Noah faked a grimace. "That's what he wanted you to play last year when you got mad and quit."

"Funny, isn't it? And this year I don't mind. I can't believe it."

Noah smiled. "I can believe it. Natural running speed runs in the family and that's what a fielder needs. Now, should you fold your share of the laundry without being reminded — that would be unbelievable."

Max entered the family room. The coffee cup in his hand steamed.

"Great stuff, Adam," he said, as the boy passed him on his way to the basement. To Noah, he added "And the provincial finals coming up. You've come a long way, big guy."

"Thanks, Uncle Coffee."

"Coach got you on some fine-tuning drills these last few days? Two weeks to go?"

"Two weeks Thursday. And no. Coach wasn't at track either Tuesday or Thursday this week. He had to go in to have tests done on his knee."

Max stopped slurping at his coffee. "He been having problems?"

Noah shrugged. "It's been off and on for almost a year now. He figures it's just cartilage. They can cut in and remove it and he'll be back running in a week."

"Guy like that — running means so much. Hope he's right."

Adam came up from the basement laundry room carrying a basket of unfolded clothes.

"Ya wanta watch a left fielder fold laundry?" he said.

"Unbelievable!" replied Noah.

* * *

Later that afternoon, Noah went to the Civic Stadium for what was supposed to be his weekly speed workout.

"Buchan's not here again," Diane said, when Noah emerged from the change room.

"He's in hospital," said Marc.

"His knee?" Noah asked. He had hated hospitals every since his father had gotten sick.

"Yeah. But maybe more."

"Whadyamean? He told me it was just cartilage. That they'd scrape it clean and he'd be back running."

Marc shrugged. "Nobody knows for sure."

The three friends jogged easily through a three-kilometre warm-up. They tried doing 200-metre intervals: running 200-metres at almost full speed, concentrating on smooth form as Buchan had taught them, then jogging easily for 200 metres to recover. When Buchan had them run this workout, they did twelve repeats. Only the last two really hurt.

That was Buchan's coaching secret. He would have them do set repeats of various distances. He would tell them how fast to run each, how long to spend in a recovery jog. And it always seemed too easy — until the last two or three repeats, which took race-like effort to maintain pace.

But today the fun had disappeared. Without Buchan to tease them, urge them on, they all found it difficult to focus. After six repeat intervals, they decided to start the warm-down.

Later, while they stretched on the infield grass, Diane made a suggestion. "Hey, guys, why don't we meet tomorrow after school and go visit Buchan in the hospital? We've only got a couple of weeks before the provincial finals. I think we could all use a lift right about now."

She was right. But what they got was not exactly a lift.

17

Buchan's Bad News

Diane, Marc, and Noah pushed onto the hospital elevator. Each clutched a bouquet of flowers.

"Hope he's got something to put these in," said Diane.

"Maybe he could hold them in his teeth," joked Marc.

Diane and Marc laughed together, much to the discomfort of others in the elevator. It was late afternoon, nearly meal time. Noah could smell the meal carts in the corridors, and the familiar mixture of antiseptic, medicine, and flowers. The bell dinged, the elevator doors opened, and they scurried out in search of Room 452.

"That's gonna be my time in the provincial finals," Diane said. "A personal best by eleven seconds."

Marc laughed. "Noah and I have to do even better," he said. "That is, knock another twenty seconds off our time to have a hope of finishing in the top three."

Noah looked at him. "You mean run under 4:20?" he said, his disbelief showing on his face.

Marc nodded. "That's what it'll take to win."

"I'm just thrilled to be running the finals," Noah replied.

"That doesn't sound like a winner's thinking to me," said Diane. Then she turned and put a finger to her lips, for they had carried this conversation down the corridor and right into Room 452.

Buchan was asleep, propped up in the hospital bed, a book facedown on the bedclothes over his chest. His head lolled to one side. He was snoring lightly.

"Should we wake him?" whispered Diane.

"Naw. Let him sleep. Let's look for something to put these flowers in," Diane said.

A quick but quiet search turned up nothing until Diane appealed to the nursing station. A volunteer worker rustled up one vase, big enough for the bouquets.

As they leaned on the window sill to sign their cards, Buchan awoke. "Hi, guys. I must have dozed off for a minute."

"It must be the age thing again," said Marc, teasing.

"It certainly isn't the mileage I'm putting in these days," Buchan replied with a weak smile. Noah stood in the corner, partially hidden behind the door. "You can come in, too, Noah," Buchan said. "I won't let the bedclothes bite."

Noah smiled wanly. He was too familiar with the hospital. He had sat on the edge of a bed just like Buchan's too many times, had stared out the window at the parking lot below many, many afternoons.

"I'm okay," Noah replied.

"They treating you okay?" asked Diane.

"I'll bet the meals are not anything to write home about," said Marc, before Buchan could reply. "I have an uncle who spent a week in here. He said the meals would starve a barber's pole." He laughed. "Whatever that is."

"Barber's pole?" repeated Diane. "That's that thing like a fence post with the candy stripes around it. It came from the days when barbers cut hair and did surgery. You know, removed your appendix and stuff."

Buchan looked up from his bed. "That's a nice thought," he said.

"Yeah," said Marc. "Like, a nice trim around the ears, even up the sideburns, and go heavy on the tonsils." They all laughed, especially Marc.

An awkward silence followed. Finally, Diane spoke.

"How's the leg?"

Buchan's eyes moved down the bed to his knee. "They're still doing tests. It's apparently a little more complicated than we thought."

"You're going to be all right, aren't you?" Noah blurted. "I mean … "

Buchan shifted in the bed, and took a deep breath before he replied. "We'll know when the tests come back." His voice sounded like crumpled paper, like there was a pain in his throat that he couldn't swallow. He was silent for a minute. "If it's what the doctor thinks, they may have to amputate," he continued softly. A small tear formed in the corner of his eye. "I'm sorry. I'm not very good company today." He reached for the call cord pinned to his pillow. "You'll have to excuse me now."

The nurse arrived, and Noah, Diane, and Marc were politely but firmly ushered out.

At the elevator, they met Bill Judge. He wore a crisp business suit and his reflecting sunglasses, even though he was indoors.

"How is he?" Judge asked.

"Kinda choked up. He said they might have to amputate."

Bill Judge took off his sunglasses. It was only the second time Noah had seen him do so. "Yeah, it could be worse than that," he said.

"What do you mean?" replied Noah.

Judge fidgeted for a second, looked at Noah, then at Diane and Marc, then at the floor. "Look, I like this guy," he said. "He's the best coach I ever had."

"We know that," said Marc.

"His wife said there are two possibilities. They think it might be cancer. If so, they'll likely amputate. If it's a benign growth, they'll try to save the knee. In that case he'll be in a cast for a few weeks at most."

Judge looked up, holding Noah's gaze. "In any event, he'll never run again."

* * *

Noah walked home the ten blocks from the hospital. He had not felt so depressed since his father died. He stumbled along, block after block, oblivious to the cars and people around him.

Running with Buchan, he had started to feel normal for the first time in two years. And now, he realized, Buchan might die too. Nobody said that, but when adults talked about cancer that's what they meant.

As Noah walked by the corner store, Rhonda Rogers snapped her bubblegum at him. She was dressed in a black top and black shorts, her dyed black hair pulled viciously to one side. Her black lipstick bracketed what might have been a smile. Ian Brant and Neil Zeko stood up from where they sat by the store's bicycle rack. Neil took a drink from the pop can in his hand.

"It's lover boy, everybody," Ian said, laughing. "He's gonna marry the track star and go to the Olympics."

"Let's see how fast he can run now!" said Ian. He was taller and heavier than Noah and Neil. He had tied his shirt around his waist to show off his tan. He took five quick steps toward Noah.

This time, Noah didn't move. "What do you want?" he said, looking up from his sorrow. "Or are you just being your normal jerk self?"

Ian stopped directly in front of Noah, leaned his nose almost against his. "Pretty sassy for a sissy," he said. "I hear your coach is sick."

Neil sauntered up. "Should we teach him a lesson?" He sipped at his pop can again, then reared back in mock surprise and spat the pop out on the edge of the road. "Oh, his coach is sick, is he? That's sad, that's really sad and I'm all broken up."

Rhonda rose and started off down the street. "You have to be the biggest jerk I know," she said to Neil. "What do you do, go to jerk school or something?"

If Noah was puzzled by this outburst, Neil and Ian were stunned. They ignored Noah and stood silently watching as Rhonda stomped away. Noah even thought she offered him a thin smile as she went by.

18

Noah Quits Track

Wednesday of the next week, Noah made his announcement at the dinner table.

"I'm quitting track," he said.

Mrs. Meyers brought her fork halfway to her mouth, then put it down again.

"You don't mean that," she said.

"I just don't care any more," replied Noah. "I did care. I thought. Maybe I was just running away from things. Really."

Max came in from the side kitchen door, carrying a plastic dish filled with homemade chocolate chip cookies. He shivered, and rubbed his hands together. "Whoever would've thought we'd get frost in June?" he asked.

"Did we?" Adam inquired.

"Not yet. But if it stays clear tonight, better cover those tomato plants."

"Noah said he's not running in the provincial finals," Mrs. Meyers said. "He's quit running."

"Quit?" Max's voice showed his surprise.

Noah, wordless, nodded.

"But why?"

"I … " Noah halted, a pain in his throat. "I don't need a reason. I just don't care."

"He hasn't trained for more than a week. Just sits in his room and mopes."

"I am not moping. I'm reading. Or is that not allowed now?"

"Romance gone sour?" Max said, teasing. When that elicited no hint of a smile, he retracted, became more serious.

"What's your coach say about this?" he asked.

"He ... doesn't know."

"Well, surely he will find out sometime, won't he? I mean, come the day of the race? When's that, a week Saturday? You going to wait until then to tell him?"

Mrs. Meyers turned to Max. "John Buchan's in the hospital."

"That true, Noah?"

Noah nodded, unable to voice an answer.

"He going to be out for the big race?"

Noah shrugged.

"You been to see him? What's his trouble?" asked Mrs. Meyers.

"I ... Diane and Marc and I went to see him." Noah was having trouble with his voice.

"What did he say?" asked Mrs. Meyers.

"He was too busy to talk much." Noah wiped away a tear.

"I think you should talk this over with him," said Max. "I really do."

Noah stood up. "It's just none of your business," he said, angrily. "And I would appreciate it if you'd all just butt out. You're always over here, butting in. Just leave me alone! Get a life!" Noah's voice had turned frosty. He stomped from the kitchen. His heavy feet clumped on the stairs to his room.

* * *

Later that evening, Mrs. Meyers knocked softly on Noah's door.

"Go away."

"I just need a minute."

"I can hear you fine from there."

"Yeah? Well, I can't hear you. I'd like to talk to you. Face to face. Please."

"It's not locked."

Noah lay sprawled across the bed, an unread book open on the floor. His mother sat down beside him.

"I'm sorry about your coach."

"It's not your fault."

"Who're you mad at?"

"I'm not mad."

Noah shifted on the bed.

"Remember when Adam pulled that tantrum last fall over being sent to left field? He didn't think he was angry about anything else."

"Well, nobody's benched me."

"No. You've benched yourself. Just like Adam did. So who's angry now? Are you trying to get even with your coach for getting sick?"

"He's not sick. He's … he needs an operation."

"So? This'll really show him. It sounds to me like you're the one who's angry, but at whom?"

Noah swiped at a tear with the back of his wrist. "He didn't have to die! He didn't have to die!"

"So don't run the race on Saturday. He'll know better next time!"

Noah looked up. He swabbed at his tears with the back of his wrist.

"It does sound silly, doesn't it?" he said. His mother smiled, and gave him a quick hug.

"Remember that picture you brought home from the store last year?" she asked.

"The one with Bill Judge and Dad?"

"Take another close look."

Noah lifted his eyes to the spot on the wall beside his bed. Bill Judge was still lunging over the finish line. His father was caught forever in the click of a stopwatch. "What?" he asked.

His mother pointed to the third man, the one in the foreground with his back to the camera. The man crouched, his fists in balls, his shouting face contorted.

Noah looked closer. He was twenty years younger, as was everyone in the photograph. But there was no mistaking him. The man in the foreground was John Buchan.

"I'll let you spend some time alone," she said. "You have to do what is right for you."

* * *

After school the next day, Thursday, Noah walked to the hospital and took the elevator to the fourth floor.

He paused for a moment at the entrance to the room. He remembered Diane's prediction regarding the race: 4:52.

Buchan was sitting up in bed reading when Noah entered. "Hi kid!" he said, some of the sparkle back in his voice. "How ya been?"

Noah moved toward the side of the bed. "I've got something I want you to have a look at," he said. He pulled the photograph out of the plastic bag he had been carrying. "Remember this?" Noah asked.

Buchan held the picture at arm's length, then reached for his glasses. "Well, I'll be," he said, letting out a tuneless whistle.

"That's ... that's Bill Judge. That was, let me see, 1979, the year he finished second in the provincials. And this," he said, tapping the glass on the picture, "was the day he qualified, with a better time than won the provincials."

"I bet he felt bad."

"Not as bad as I did. See, that's me, there, in the foreground. I was his coach."

"I know."

"See, if I hadn't been so intense, he'd have won the provincial title that year. He might have set a record. But I over-trained him, pushed him too hard. He left his best race on the practice field." Buchan looked once more at the photograph. "Oh, yeah! And that guy with the stop watch … "

"I know. That's my dad. Funny, isn't it?"

Buchan smiled again at the picture, then turned to Noah. "What's this I hear about you quitting the club?"

"I … I haven't quit the club. I," Noah stared at the floor. "I just skipped a few workouts."

"Your coach isn't there for a couple of weeks and you figure you can take it easy?" Buchan was smiling.

"I felt … bad. About you."

Buchan stroked his chin. "Look, Noah. I've been feeling sorry enough for myself. I don't need extra help. If you want to do something for me, even out of pity, you can."

"What's that?"

"Run the provincials on Saturday. The 1500-metre. Or the 3000. Or both. You qualified. Just run them. Then, if you feel like quitting, I'll help you write your resignation letter."

"Letter?"

"Just kidding. Quit now, you'll let your teammates down. You'll let your coach down. You'll let yourself down, most of all. You put a lot of work into getting this far."

"It's not the same without you there," Noah said.

"As a coach, I hope I've helped you a bit. But the things that matter you have to do for yourself. You're not running for me. There will always be something that comes along that you can use as an excuse for not finishing what you started."

"Are you going to be okay?" Noah asked.

"The doctors haven't decided what to do yet. They'll either amputate, or dig out the growth — whatever it is — and slap my whole leg in a big thick cast. Then, nobody knows." Buchan looked at Noah directly. For once his silver tooth did not sparkle. "Look. It's not very often a coach gets a runner capable of winning a provincial title. Last time I did was twenty years ago. This year, either you or Marc could do it."

Noah blinked, as though he had not thought of this possibility.

"I can't beat Marc," he said.

"Not if you think you can't," Buchan replied. "You're running your first year as a midget, and this is Marc's final. Next year, he moves up to juvenile. Sure he's got an advantage — and the experience from last year."

"I'm not sure I want to," said Noah.

Buchan leaned forward and pointed a finger at Noah. "I know your Dad died of cancer," he said. "And maybe I've got cancer and maybe I don't. But you can't run away from a challenge because your coach got sick."

Noah squirmed. "Sounds stupid when you put it that way," he replied.

"We all do stupid things sometimes. Your father would have been proud of what you've done this year," Buchan went on. "He'd have been insufferably proud. Heck, I'm insufferably proud. So do me one favour. If you won't run the race for me, and you won't run it for your dad, then run it for the experience."

"But I haven't trained in almost two weeks," Noah replied. "I haven't got a chance."

Buchan scoffed. "Two weeks off isn't going to hurt. Not at your age. You're in great shape. You don't lose it that fast. Besides," he added, "at this point it's all up here." He pointed to his greying temple. "Behave yourself the first lap and you'll have enough left for a fast finish."

Noah paused and looked Buchan in the eye. "I'll run," he said, finally. But his voice was flat, as though John Buchan had just asked him to complete an unwelcome chore.

Later, in the corridor at the end of the hall, Noah stood waiting for the elevator. He shuffled his feet. Three other people, an elderly man and a middle-aged couple, were also waiting. No one talked. Noah watched the floor indicator. One, two, three, four ...

A bell dinged, and the doors opened with a squishy sound. Out stepped Rhonda Rogers and Neil Zeko. Noah didn't know what to expect when he saw the pair. Certainly not what happened next.

"Hi," said Rhonda, quiet, subdued. Neil nodded to Noah, and mumbled a greeting.

"Did you see him?" Rhonda asked. Her usually lilting voice sounded flat. She wore no makeup. Instead of her in-your-face wardrobe, she wore denim jeans and a blue denim jacket. She still wore the stud in her left nostril.

"Who? You mean the coach?" Noah replied.

"Yeah," said Rhonda. "He's my uncle. Mom says they may have to amputate his leg."

Noah looked from Rhonda to Neil. He could see the fear in their eyes.

"My track coach is your uncle?" he asked.

"He's a good guy," said Neil. "This sucks."

"My mother and step-father get on my case, but Uncle John just laughs and says they'll grow out of it. He's a great uncle."

"He's a great coach, too."

Rhonda touched Noah's arm. "Look," she said. "When Mom told me Uncle John had cancer I cried all night. And I got thinking about you. And how your father died of cancer and all. I didn't have any idea of how you must have felt until now."

19

Noah Shows Up

A crowd of more than 1000 filled the grandstand at Oshawa Civic Fields the day of the provincial finals. Max, Mrs. Meyers, and Adam were among them.

Down on the track, Noah wandered the infield, looking for a familiar face. He stepped around athletes stretching, side-stepped others in warm-up jogs, and avoided some in mid-stride. Then he almost tripped over two pair of legs sprawled in his path.

"Hey, watch where you're goin', Meyers," said Ian Brant. "You don't own the place, you know."

Ian and Neil Zeko lay sprawled out on the grass in an area reserved for athletes. Neil was blowing bubblegum bubbles.

"Where's your girlfriend, lover boy?" Ian taunted. "Or does she know your name yet?"

At that moment, Bill Judge walked up.

"Well. There you are, Meyers. I've been looking for you at track for the past two weeks."

"Sorry."

Judge turned to Ian and Neil. "You guys should not be here," he said. "This area's reserved for athletes."

"Oh, ath-el-eetes like Meyers," said Ian, sarcastically.

"We're waiting for a friend," said Neil. "She said to meet us here."

"Well, you guys should wait up there in the stands. Only athletes and their coaches are allowed down here."

"You don't call Meyers an athlete, do you?" retorted Ian.

"Come on, Ian," said Neil. "Knock it off. You know. I told you his coach was Rhonda's uncle."

"Oh, yeah."

"Yeah, I call Meyers an athlete," replied Judge. "Now move your butts, both of you."

Ian and Neil got to their feet and turned to go. They shuffled off along the backfield fence. After a few paces, Neil turned back to Noah. "Good luck," he said. "Rhonda said she hopes you do well, too."

"Thanks."

"You all set?" Bill Judge asked Noah.

"Not as set as I'd like to be. I kinda goofed up this last couple of weeks," Noah replied.

"Well, maybe it's better than *over*-training."

"Any word about coach Buchan?"

Judge turned partly away. "They still haven't decided. Last night they were talking about amputation."

"When'll we know?"

"I'll go see him later today. After the meet." An awkward silence followed. Finally, Judge referred to his clipboard. "Your 1500-metre race is in half an hour. This thing with Buchan has hit us all. I can understand how you feel. I'm glad you've decided to run today."

"Thanks."

"Yeah. Coupla other things." Judge removed his sunglasses. "I know I sounded kind of cheesed off when you left the sprinters' group to join Buchan. You were beginning to show some promise. Then, when you told me you were going to leave the group, I gave you a hard time."

"That's all right."

"Well, no. I'm sorry for being so tough. I thought you were a quitter, but you've proved me wrong. No hard feelings?"

"None."

"And one other thing." Judge lifted his hand and put his sunglasses back on. "Just remember, every race at every distance comes down to a sprint. You'll be in a real race today, and it will come down to the last 200 metres. No matter how hard you work for the first 1300, it won't mean anything if you don't have a fast finish."

"I hear you."

"So remember those sprint drills. I'll be at the 200-metre mark. You see me, you'll know it's time to lift those knees, pump those arms."

"Pump! Lift! Boy, do I remember that! Yeah, thanks — Bill."

Judge grasped Noah's hand and smiled. For the first time since Noah had known him, he wore a big, wide, white-toothed grin. "Do great out there," he said. "You've got stuff you've never even used before."

Judge looked up as Diane and Marc jogged over. "Okay, people. Diane, your race doesn't begin for another two hours. Sit down and relax. You two guys," he said, motioning to Noah and Marc with his clipboard, "should get started. Don't overdo the warm-up. Do stretches, keep loose. I'll keep you posted about start time."

* * *

Together, Noah and Marc jogged slowly around the track perimeter. Racers from other events flew by.

"I missed you at the track," Marc said.

"I'll tell you about it later," Noah replied. "I had to work out a whole lot of things. After we visited Buchan in the hospital I decided to quit."

"Doesn't look like you've quit to me."

"I've missed two weeks of training. I'm just here to finish. Going for a win is out of the question."

Marc shrugged. "Me, I'm going all out. Next year I'll be sixteen and have to run with the juveniles, so the going gets tougher. Wish me luck."

Noah and Marc continued the rest of their warm-up in silence.

Finally, Judge came across the infield to where they were stretching. "Fifteen minutes," he said. Then, he lifted his sunglasses to his forehead and smiled. "Good luck. Either of you can win this race. Now, one of you go out there and do it."

Behind them, a work crew had opened a large gate behind the 100-metre starting blocks to let a big passenger van through to the side of the track, but Noah and Marc were too nervous to notice.

20

A Fast Finish

Mark!"
Ten runners tensed, toes to the line, coiled.
BANG!

Ten runners sprang forward, jostling in the first few strides, each seeking best position. All had qualified in regional run-offs, as had Noah and Marc. And Jamie Green. All were fast. Any one of them could win the race.

Marc surged ahead early, stepping clearly out in front by the 100-metre mark. Half a pace behind him was Jamie Green, still dressed in his signature colour. He had won their regional final with a time of 4:29. Right on their heels was a runner from the western region, in black.

Already two yards behind came a runner in blue and, another stride back, one in maroon. By the 300-metre mark, with three laps to go, they had settled into order: Marc, in Viking orange, followed by White, Green, Black, Blue, and Maroon. Noah Meyers, also in Viking orange, was in seventh place.

" … Fifty-one, fifty-two, fifty-three, fifty-four … "

Noah could hear the cheers in the stands. His eyes were focused on the track and on the back of a maroon racing top, now ten metres ahead.

Viking sprinters had gathered along the infield side of the back straight. They yelled encouragement to Marc. At the middle of the top bend Noah could see Judge.

"Hang in there, Meyers!" he yelled. "Don't lose contact!"

During the second lap, Noah noticed the crowd shift as a large passenger van pulled slowly closer to the edge of the track at the end of the front straight.

On the track, the runner in black, who had challenged Marc for the lead, began to struggle. He fell back quickly; by the time they hit the front straight, with two laps to go, two runners had passed him. Blue and Maroon.

Noah caught the runner in black as they entered the top corner. The quick early pace of the leaders was starting to take its toll.

" … 2:03, 2:04, 2:05 … "

Noah now moved into fifth place, five metres behind the runner in maroon. Marc had clearly moved to the front, passing Jamie Green by a full ten metres. He was running away with the race.

"Vi-king! Vi-king! Vi-king!"

Viking team members lined the inside of the back straight, their cheers for Marc urging Noah as well. He had run loosely so far. Now, as he entered the back straight, the strain of the race began.

His lungs burned. His legs had gained weight. Although he had started modestly, he knew the second lap was faster than the first. Even though he was well back from the leaders he was still running over his head, faster than he ever had before. The bear on his back would grow larger. Soon.

Starting down the back straight, he moved to the right to go around the runner in blue. Fourth place. Fourth place.

 "Vi-king! Vi-king! Vi-king!"

Passing Blue, Noah could see the length of the track. Judge, his arms flailing, his sunglasses gone, cheered them on with a deep, full voice. At the corner of the grandstand, even Ian Brant and Neil Zeko were jumping up and down, their arms flapping.

"Get 'em, Marc! Go get 'em, Marc!"

Suddenly, Noah could see the wheelchair beside the outside lane. A man in a Viking jacket with a balding head and wire-rim glasses was in it. Rhonda Rogers, still with black lipstick, was behind it. Coach John Buchan, his huge thick leg in cast thrust straight out before him, was the man in the wheelchair.

"Atta boy, Noah!" Buchan yelled. "Looking smooth, looking smooth. Reel 'em in! One and a half laps. Reel 'em in, Noah!"

Noah could not hear him in the roar. But from the movement of Buchan's arms, he recognized the casting motion, the small circling turn of his coach's right hand that meant: reel 'em in, reel 'em in.

Noah saw the leg, and in his head he heard the voice. The hurt began in his throat. The tears swelled in his eyes. And the bear fell off his back. With a smirk of a smile and a slight wave, he was past Buchan, and at the same time swept past the runner in blue to third place.

Surging down the front straight, Noah surprised himself by passing Marc, whose strong easy stride had been reduced to a struggle. His early pace had taken its toll. Noah was in second place.

DING-A-LING-A-LING.

" ... 3:13, 3:14, 3:15 ... "

Bell lap. One lap to go, Noah told himself.

Jamie Green's back, ten metres ahead, was now Noah's only target. Not coming back any more. Not moving away, either. They rounded the top turn, going into the back straight. Noah hurt. The easy gains had all been won. He would have to work hard for every step now.

On the infield side along the back straight he could see the Clarington Viking sprinters gathered: Ryan, Jason, Melissa, Mandy. They blended their voices now to urge him on.

"Mey-ers! Mey-ers! Mey-ers!"

"Vi-king! Vi-king! Vi-king!"

Three-hundred metres to go. Ten metres back.

Buchan had turned his wheelchair to see better. He waved his Viking jacket in circles over his head, yelling. Rhonda Rogers, behind her uncle, ducked the jacket, and cheered into the wall of white noise.

For you, Coach, Noah said to himself. For you, Dad.

At that moment, Judge leaned over the track's edge, just beyond the 200-metre mark. His voice was lost in the roaring crowd. He lifted his arms, his legs, in pantomime. Noah could read his lips and in his head heard the voice in the sprinter drills: 'Pump those arms! Lift those legs! Pump! Lift! Pump! Lift!'

Two-hundred metres to go. He was now down to one last sprint. Noah pumped his arms, lifted his knees high, and powered around the turn, pump, lift, pump, lift. He came off the bend two metres back. With 100 metres to go, he rose up even higher on his toes, his arms pumping high, his knees lifted, the wind in his face and the roar of the crowd surrounding him, pushing him forward.

He pulled even with Jamie Green, dared not to look sideways, focused straight ahead. Coach, Coach, Coach, Dad, Dad, Dad, he chanted in his head.

" … 4:19, 4:20, 4:21 … "

Noah pulled ahead of Green on the last step, and won, with a time of four minutes, nineteen seconds.

Noah fell on the track then, crying, his lungs sucking air for oxygen. Finally, an arm reached down to pull him to his feet. Jamie Green offered a hand and mumbled congratulations. Around him, everyone was jumping up and down, and extending their hands. Marc was there, and Diane, and other runners.

Noah couldn't believe he did it, couldn't believe he won the provincial title, couldn't believe that Coach Buchan made it. He waved to the stands. He thought he could make out Adam, and his mother, and Max.

But first he headed for the far corner.

Noah caught sight of the wheelchair while it was still on the track. Wordless, he ran to Buchan, exchanged a high-five which ended with their hands gripped together.

"You done real good, Noah," Buchan said. "Way to go, champ. You made your old coach proud."

21

Keep On Running

His mother was there, as well as Max and Adam. There were hugs all around, and congratulations.

"You hit a homer, big bro!" Adam exclaimed.

"Great race, Noah," said Max.

"I am proud of you," said his mother.

Noah dragged them halfway around the track. "There's a guy you have to meet," he said.

"Mom, Max. This is John Buchan."

Buchan shook hands. "And this is Adam?" he asked, surprising Adam with a handshake as well. Rhonda stood behind her uncle. She smiled at Noah.

Buchan turned to Mrs. Meyers. "You must be very proud of this guy. That was one powerful run out there."

"We are," said Mrs. Meyers.

"He had an excellent coach," said Max.

"Well, that run took a lot of guts."

"When the going gets tough, the tough get going," replied Max.

"Spare us the clichés, uncle," said Adam, with a grin.

"But he's right," said Buchan. "Winners are those who give full throttle when the bear's on their back."

"Or after they hit the wall," said Noah. "Speaking of which, Coach, how about you?"

"We still don't know," replied Buchan. "But after talking to you the other day, I figured I couldn't go on feeling sorry for myself. Losing a leg didn't stop Terry Fox. Or Rick Hansen."

"Who're they?" asked Adam.

"You know. Terry Fox. He's the guy who ran halfway across Canada on one leg. Rick Hansen traveled around the world by wheelchair," said Max.

Buchan smiled, his silver tooth gleaming in the sun. "Now do me a favour. Keep at it. Be the best you can be. Your uncle can't have all the clichés."

"Somebody has to do those long Sunday runs," said Noah.

"And if I remember correctly, you have an hour before the 5000. You're fit enough to run that, too, and you qualified. You need to jog down, do a bit of stretching, get ready."

"Will you be here?"

"I gotta get back. You have no idea how many favours I had to cash to get down here in time. But I'll be thinking of you. If you try hard, you'll see me at the 200-metre mark every lap."

Rhonda helped her uncle turn the wheelchair. Then she looked at Noah.

"Way to go," she said, smiling.

"Neil and Ian are over in the grandstand, I think," Noah said.

"I saw them. Thanks."

Then Marc was in front of Noah, grinning. Beside him was Diane. Diane gave Noah a long hug and kissed him on one cheek, then the other. "Maybe something will rub off for my race," she said.

Marc offered a high-five. "Whatta run!" he said.

Noah turned to his friend. "How'd you do?"

"Third. Bronze. I was dying out there after the first two laps. Then I saw you turn on the burners on lap three so I put on a surge. Still ran a 4:22 — my personal best by ten seconds."

"I never would have done it if you hadn't burned everybody off early."

"Yeah, Buddy, but you had the fast finish. You earned it."

An hour later, when the gun sounded to start the 5000, Noah toed the line. He danced easily into the lead by the 200-metre mark, then he settled into an easy pace, letting other runners use up their energy to pass him. There'll be time enough to catch them later, he thought.

He ran smoothly, his long legs flying, his breath deep and even. He could run all day.

Other books you'll enjoy in the Sports Stories series...

Baseball

☐ *Curve Ball* by John Danakas #1
Tom Poulos is looking forward to a summer of baseball in Toronto until his mother puts him on a plane to Winnipeg.

☐ *Baseball Crazy* by Martyn Godfrey #10
Rob Carter wins an all-expenses-paid chance to be batboy at the Blue Jays' spring training camp in Florida.

☐ *Shark Attack* by Judi Peers #25
The East City Sharks have a good chance of winning the county championship until their arch rivals get a tough new pitcher.

Basketball

☐ *Fast Break* by Michael Coldwell #8
Moving from Toronto to small-town Nova Scotia was rough, but when Jeff makes the school basketball team he thinks things are looking up.

☐ *Camp All-Star* by Michael Coldwell #12
In this insider's view of a basketball camp, Jeff Lang encounters some unexpected challenges.

☐ *Nothing but Net* by Michael Coldwell #18
The Cape Breton Grizzly Bears face an out-of-town basketball tournament they're sure to lose.

☐ *Slam Dunk* by Steven Barwin and Gabriel David Tick #23
In this sequel to *Roller Hockey Blues*, Mason Ashbury's basketball team adjusts to the arrival of some new players: girls.

Figure Skating

☐ *A Stroke of Luck* by Kathryn Ellis #6
Strange accidents are stalking one of the skaters at the Millwood Arena.

☐ *The Winning Edge* by Michele Martin Bosley #28
Jennie wants more than anything to win a grueling series of competitions, but is success worth losing her friends?

Gymnastics

☐ *The Perfect Gymnast* by Michele Martin Bossley #9
Abby's new friend has all the confidence she needs, but she also has a serious problem that nobody but Abby seems to know about.

Ice hockey

☐ *Shoot to Score* by Sandra Richmond #31
Playing defence on the B list, alongside the coach's mean-spirited son, are tough obstacles for Steven to overcome, but he perseveres and changes his luck.

☐ *Two Minutes for Roughing* by Joseph Romain #2
As a new player on a tough Toronto hockey team, Les must fight to fit in.

☐ *Hockey Night in Transcona* by John Danakas #7
Cody Powell gets promoted to the Transcona Sharks' first line, bumping out the coach's son who's not happy with the change.

☐ *Face Off* by C.A. Forsyth #13
A talented hockey player finds himself competing with his best friend for a spot on a select team.

☐ *Hat Trick* by Jacqueline Guest #20
The only girl on an all-boys' hockey team works to earn the captain's respect and her mother's approval.

☐ *Hockey Heroes* by John Danakas #22
A left-winger on the thirteen-year-old Transcona Sharks adjusts to a new best friend and his mom's boyfriend.

☐ *Hockey Heat Wave* by C.A. Forsyth #27
In this sequel to *Face Off*, Zack and Mitch encounter some trouble when it looks like only one of them will make the select team at hockey camp.

Riding

☐ *A Way With Horses* by Peter McPhee #11
A young Alberta rider invited to study show jumping at a posh local riding school uncovers a secret.

☐ *Riding Scared* by Marion Crook #15
A reluctant new rider struggles to overcome her fear of horses.

☐ *Katie's Midnight Ride* by C.A. Forsyth #16
An ambitious barrel racer finds herself without a horse weeks before her biggest rodeo.

☐ *Glory Ride* by Tamara L. Williams #21
Chloe Anderson fights memories of a tragic fall for a place on the Ontario Young Riders' Team.

☐ *Cutting it Close* by Marion Crook #24
In this novel about barrel racing, a talented young rider finds her horse is in trouble just as she is about to compete in an important event.

Roller hockey

☐ *Roller Hockey Blues* by Steven Barwin and Gabriel David Tick #17
Mason Ashbury faces a summer of boredom until he makes the roller-hockey team.

Running

☐ *Fast Finish* by Bill Swan #30
Noah is a promising young runner headed for the provincial finals when he suddenly decides to withdraw from the event.

Sailing

☐ *Sink or Swim* by William Pasnak #5
Dario can barely manage the dog paddle, but thanks to his mother he's spending the summer at a water sports camp.

Soccer

☐ *Lizzie's Soccer Showdown* by John Danakas #3
When Lizzie asks why the boys and girls can't play together, she finds herself the new captain of the soccer team.

Swimming

☐ *Breathing Not Required* by Michele Martin Bossley #4
An eager synchronized swimmer works hard to be chosen for a solo and almost loses her best friend in the process.

☐ *Water Fight!* by Michele Martin Bossley #14
Josie's perfect sister is driving her crazy but when she takes up swimming — Josie's sport — it's too much to take.

☐ *Taking a Dive* by Michele Martin Bossley #19
Josie holds the provincial record for the butterfly, but in this sequel to *Water Fight*, she can't seem to match her own time and might not go on to the nationals.

☐ *Great Lengths* by Sandra Diersch #26
Fourteen-year-old Jessie decides to find out whether the rumours about a new swimmer at her Vancouver club are true.

Track and Field

☐ *Mikayla's Victory* by Cynthia Bates #29
Mikayla must compete against her friend if she wants to represent her school at an important track event.